Michael Page lives in Australia. This is his thirteenth novel.

MY ANASTASIA

As the First World War rages, Lieutenant Benjamin Knyve and shipmate Stefan Carter enter revolutionary Russia to protect the royal family from Communist captivity. But they succeed in saving only the grievously wounded youngest daughter, Anastasia, from the murderous revolutionaries. Embarking on a thousand-mile dash to safety, Benjamin must confront those who might betray Anastasia, deal with her drug dependency and accept the strange result of her pregnancy. Faced with the tragedy of war, will the couple ever find a solution to their problem?

MICHAEL PAGE

◆

MY ANASTASIA

Complete and Unabridged

ULVERSCROFT
Leicester

First published in Great Britain in 2004 by
Robert Hale Limited
London

First Large Print Edition
published 2005
by arrangement with
Robert Hale Limited
London

British Library CIP Data

Page, Michael F., *1922 –*
My Anastasia.—Large print ed.—
Ulverscroft large print series: adventure & suspense
1. Princesses—Russia—Fiction 2. Russia—History—
Nicholas II, *1894 – 1917*—Fiction
3. Historical fiction 4. Large type books
I. Title
823.9'14 [F]

ISBN 1–84617–061–3

Published by
F. A. Thorpe (Publishing)
Anstey, Leicestershire

Set by Words & Graphics Ltd.
Anstey, Leicestershire
Printed and bound in Great Britain by
T. J. International Ltd., Padstow, Cornwall

This book is printed on acid-free paper

1

The doctor said, 'He's gone,' and closed the wrinkled eyelids. 'Remarkable old chap, eh? Well over his century.'

Martin Knyve, great-grandson and sole descendant of Captain Benjamin Knyve RN, DSO, DSC, nodded politely. He and old Benjamin had not been close, perhaps because Martin was a solicitor in Norwich and the captain despised lawyers.

Martin made all the necessary arrangements and cleared the captain's possessions from his room in the Fowlers Haven Retirement Home. They included a stack of foolscap written in Benjamin's small neat hand. Martin glanced through the papers, took them home with him, and told his wife, 'I'd better wade through the old boy's memoirs.'

Captain Knyve's story began: I first met the Grand Duchess Anastasia Romanov, youngest daughter of Nicholas the Emperor of All the Russias, when she was just ten years old. That was in the summer of 1911, when I was five years older and had no interest in little girls. I had recently graduated from the

Royal Naval Cadet College in Dartmouth and completed my cruise in the training ship, and I was on leave while I awaited appointment as midshipman in the Navy. I was following in the footsteps of numerous predecessors in the Knyve family.

When my father was a young lieutenant he served a year as naval attaché to the British Embassy in Russia, then in St Petersburg. Members of the Embassy enjoyed a vigorous social life and he was invited to a ball at which he was introduced to Sophia Matislav, eldest daughter of a titled and wealthy landowner. Apparently my father and Sophia fell for each other at first glance, but Count Matislav objected to the idea of his daughter marrying a foreign officer who might whisk her away to the furthest corners of the British Empire.

Eventually he agreed to the marriage but only on condition that Sophia should visit Russia at least once a year, at his expense, accompanied by any grandchildren who might have appeared. Further, these grandchildren must be taught to write and speak Russian as well as English.

I was the youngest of Sophia's seven children, and by 1911 my siblings had long since rebelled against the count's regulations and he himself had realized they were unreasonable. But I had rather enjoyed learning Russian as well as English, and liked speaking it to my mother and accompanying her on her visits during my school summer holidays.

The 1911 visit was likely to be my last one because after that I expected Royal Navy service to stand in the way. That year one of my mother's cousins, Count Evgeni Vrybov, had invited us to stay at his summer residence at Salaskia on the Black Sea. His villa was no more than pleasant walking distance from Livadia, where the Russian imperial family had just opened their new summer palace, and Count Vrybov arranged an informal meeting with what would nowadays be known as 'the royals'. On a clear warm summer morning my mother and I and Vrybov strolled along the beach towards Livadia and soon encountered the outlying guards. They passed us through to what appeared, in the distance, to be an ordinary family enjoying a morning on the beach. As we moved closer, the Emperor Nicholas came to greet us and I was surprised by his likeness to our own King George V, who had recently ascended the throne. They were first cousins, descended from Queen Victoria, and could almost have been twin brothers. They were small, trimly built men, bearded and blue-eyed and with somewhat curt mannerisms.

Vrybov introduced us and Nicholas led us to his four daughters, Olga, Marie, Tatiana and Anastasia, who were busily constructing a large sandcastle. There was only a couple of years' difference in ages between each of the four girls, perhaps because they'd been produced in an effort to achieve a male heir to the throne. He had at last appeared in the person of Alexis, who was helping his sisters with their castle. He seemed as cheerful and agile as any other seven-year-old but he was a haemophiliac, liable to dangerous unstoppable bleeding after only a minor injury. His guardian, a hefty young sailor of the Imperial Navy, watched every move he made.

The girls curtsied to my mother and I caught one or two mischievous glances directed at me. For some reason I noticed Anastasia's very blue eyes, under thick eyebrows which almost met above her nose, and her long thick dark-blond hair. But we did not speak to each other and the meeting lasted only a few minutes before Count Vrybov eased us away.

That was my last visit to Russia before the First World War broke out in 1914 and changed the world for ever. I saw plenty of active service, including Gallipoli where I won my Distinguished Service Cross and the

Battle of Jutland where my ship, like so many British ships that day, was sunk in the North Sea and I spent hours clinging to the wreckage in the cold water.

In June 1918 I was first lieutenant of the destroyer *Javelin*, attached to the Dover Patrol. Our task was to protect the endless stream of troopships, hospital ships and supply ships, running between Britain and France, from German attack.

Dawn was just breaking one summer morning when we returned to port. I noticed a messenger bring a batch of papers aboard and a little later the skipper sent for me. He shoved a paper towards me and said, 'Orders for you, Knyve. You're to be relieved today and report immediately to Room 40Q, the Admiralty.'

The skipper didn't like me, perhaps because he was a small, cocky man and I was taller and broader than he was, or perhaps because his uniform jacket was bare of decorations and mine wore the ribbon of the DSC. When I asked rather stupidly, because it had been a long night, 'Me, sir?', he snapped, 'Yes, you, sir! And there's a hell of a lot of paperwork to clear up before you go, so you'd better get on with it.'

2

I found Room 40Q in one of the buildings commandeered by the wartime Admiralty. Its door carried the nameplate 'Captain H. Blaze, VC' and my spirits rose a little because Blaze was a family friend. When I entered he greeted me with, 'Hallo, young Benjamin. Heard from your father lately? Vice-Admiral now, isn't he?'

'Yes, sir. With the Mediterranean Fleet.'

Another man, a grey-haired civilian, was seated with his back to me. When he rose and faced me I saw he was Count Vrybov. My expression made him smile and say in Russian, 'Greetings, Benjamin. Are you surprised to see me here?'

Instinctively I replied in the same language, 'Yes, indeed I am,' and Blaze said, 'Ah — that's good. We hoped you'd still speak the language.'

I told him, 'Yes, sir. My mother likes to keep it up and I rather enjoy it. We even write to each other in Russian.'

Vrybov asked, 'You know what's happened in Russia, of course?' I nodded assent. A wartime naval officer in European waters, in those days before electronic media, often failed to see the daily newspapers but my mother had kept me well informed about the disastrous effects of the Russian revolution of 1917, especially on our family connections. I told Vrybov politely, 'But I'm glad to see you've managed to get away.'

He smiled wryly. 'I'd hardly say that. I happened to be attached to our embassy in London when the revolution broke out and I've been here ever since.'

Blaze said, 'Yes, well, that's why we're meeting today. Benjamin. I presume you know what's happened to the Russian royal family?'

Like most people I'd heard various versions of the story. The most definite seemed to be that King George had arranged for a Royal Navy ship to go to Murmansk on the Arctic Ocean, one of the few Russian ports not blockaded by the enemy, to rescue Nicholas and his family. The revolutionaries had agreed to this but some of the children had developed chickenpox and were unfit for the long journey from Moscow to Murmansk. By the time they were well again the British Labour Party had expressed violent opposition to efforts to rescue the Romanovs. Labour politicians blamed Nicholas and his wife Alexandra for oppression of the Russian working classes before the war, and for the inefficiency of the Russian command which brought defeat by Germany and allowed the German war effort to concentrate against Britain and her other allies. King George had withdrawn his offer and the revolutionaries now refused to allow Nicholas and his family to escape.

I answered Blaze with, 'Yes, sir,' and he said, 'Well, there may be another attempt to get them out of Russia.'

Rather hesitantly, and very conscious that these two middle-aged men were my superiors in rank, experience and knowledge, I offered, 'I . . . er . . . understood we'd given up trying to help the Romanovs.'

Vrybov said smoothly, 'That's the general belief. But a large portion of British society is still ready to contribute money and other assistance to freeing the Romanovs and striking a blow against the revolution. Britain and her allies have large shareholdings in Russia which will be worthless if the revolution succeeds. And abandonment of the Romanovs will have unhappy effects on . . . shall we say upper-class society in general?'

Blaze chipped in with, 'There's a possibility that loyal forces, which we call the White Army, may defeat the revolution this summer.

But there's also a danger the Bolsheviks will use the imperial family as hostages, to bargain for their own purposes.'

I'd already heard rumours that the revolution was not going too well for the Bolsheviks, which means simply 'the majority'. Later they called themselves 'communists'. But I had some doubts about the efficiency of the loyalists. One of the causes of the revolution had been that, despite the courage of the rank and file, the Russian army and bureaucracy had been riddled with corruption, jealousies and inefficiency. My mother's contacts had told her the White Army was no better.

I was beginning to understand why I'd been summoned to Room 40Q. Blaze continued with, 'Count Vrybov has asked for British help in a special mission. A naval officer would be ideal because there may be . . . well, an escape by water. And of course I remembered your Russian connections.'

Vrybov said, 'The emperor and his family have now been moved from Moscow to Tobolsk, in south-west Siberia. The Bolsheviks say the reason for this move is for their own safety, but we think it's simply to make escape, or rescue, more difficult. But Tobolsk is on the River Irtysh, running north to the Arctic Ocean, and that might be an ideal escape route.'

A naval officer does not say 'but' when he's given an order, but the order had not yet been given and I felt free to say, 'But how could one man rescue the emperor and his family?'

'There would be local help, of course. And the man we send would carry money to buy assistance, and guarantees of rewards for anyone helping him.'

Blaze and Vrybov stared at me as though expecting me to react with shouts of enthusiasm, but I asked, 'And you think I'm the right man for a job like this?'

Blaze said impatiently, 'Of course you are. You're young and strong, you've proven yourself on active service, you don't have a wife and children, and best of all you speak Russian and know something about the country and its people.'

Vrybov was nodding agreement and he added, 'And we can tell you, in strict confidence, an Allied force will soon be landing at Murmansk to protect our interests there. No doubt they'll be able to help you in various ways.'

I realized I mustn't seem to hesitate any longer. I knew that Blaze was a man of some authority in the Admiralty and if I disappointed him I might affect my future career. I said, 'Very well, then. I'll take it on.'

Blaze said, 'Good man. You could take someone with you, if we could find the right person, as a supporter. Any ideas?'

The answer sprang immediately into my mind. 'Yes — Stefan Carter. I've known him all my life and he speaks Russian too. He joined the navy when I did and he's now a leading seaman in a destroyer based on Harwich.'

Blaze began to write, saying, 'Stephen — '

'No, sir. Stefan Karnowski Carter. His mother is Russian, like mine. She came to England with Mother, as her personal maid.'

Krystyna Karnowski had eventually married my father's head gamekeeper, and Stefan was their only child. He and I grew up together and enjoyed having Russian as our 'secret language'. He joined the navy as a boy seaman when I entered as a cadet, and we'd seen each other only occasionally since then. But I knew he was the man to stand by me on a venture into danger.

Blaze said in fatherly style, 'All right, Benjamin. You'd better nip off home for a few days' leave, and Count Vrybov will contact you when we've made all the arrangements.'

3

I went home to the little seaport of Fowlers Haven, on the north-east coast of Norfolk, where the Knyves had lived for countless generations. Their names, almost obliterated by the salt winds, could be seen on many of the gravestones around the ancient church. Family legend claimed that Knyves had been pirates and smugglers before they became honest traders, until Bartholomew Knyve joined a fighting ship in the reign of George II and founded a naval dynasty. In 1806 my great-grandfather Matthew used his Trafalgar prize money to buy an estate overlooking the port, and built a house on it he named Knyve's Edge.

I could remember my mother as bright, chatty and vivacious, but war and revolution shattered her life as it shattered so many others. Of her four sons, one died on the Western Front, another in the Royal Flying Corps, and the third when his ship was torpedoed. Natasha, my oldest sister, lost her husband in the battle of the Somme and the other two lived in constant dread of the telegrams which would tell them they were war widows. My mother's brothers died in the fighting against Germany and she had heard nothing from the rest of her Russian family for more than a year.

Consequently, not wishing to add to her worries, I told her nothing about my forthcoming mission to Russia. I let her think I was on normal leave, as Stefan also did when he arrived a couple of days later and I told him a little of what lay ahead. He was a dark, wiry young man, quick to think and act, but the difference in our naval ranks caused him to be rather stiff and reserved with me until I told him to behave as though we were both civilians. He grinned with pleasure when he realized he and I would be able to spend some time in roaming over the coast and country around Fowlers Haven, as we'd done when we were boys. Outsiders might think it bleak and cold but it was our homeland.

Of course I had to tell him what little I knew about my mission, and swore him to secrecy, and asked if he'd like to join me. He agreed immediately but asked, 'Why's the navy mixed up in this?'

I'd wondered that myself, and gave him the explanation I'd worked out. 'I think King George still wants to rescue his Russian relations without causing a political uproar, and so he and his advisers have decided to do it unofficially. I knew the Blaze family has been associated with our royal family for a century or more, so that may be why Captain Blaze was drawn into it.'

We discussed it some more but I don't think we were really interested in the reasons. We were young, with the offer of adventure ahead, and we trusted our seniors knew what they were doing. And both of us had served in the Royal Navy since we were thirteen. Instant obedience to orders, and strict attention to duty, were ingrained in us.

Count Vrybov arrived a few days later, appearing without warning in a big chauffeur-driven Rolls-Royce. He gave Mama the excuse that he was on his way to visit a 'distinguished person' but could not resist the opportunity to drop in on her. She obviously thought he meant King George, whose Sandringham estate was not far from Knyve's Edge, and nodded wisely but asked no questions. A visit from her cousin was important to her and they chatted about old times, and exchanged what little information they had about aristocratic survivors of war and revolution, while he lunched with us. Afterwards he said, 'I'd just like to talk to Benjamin for a moment,' and led me to his car.

In the spacious interior he gave me a briefcase, saying, 'You'll find everything you need in here. Diplomatic passports for you and Stefan Carter, in your own names but describing you as 'Government servants'. Tickets to Bergen by sea and then by train to Stockholm where the British Embassy will make further arrangements. Travel expenses — a hundred pounds in one-pound notes.'

In those days many people did not earn a hundred pounds in a year, and somehow this knowledge impressed upon me the importance of our mission. I was even more impressed when, from another bag, Vrybov produced two money-belts and said, 'Each of these contains two hundred and fifty gold sovereigns. You'll find that gold goes a very long way in Russia these days.'

Gold coins had been withdrawn from circulation in England, to be replaced by banknotes, as soon as war broke out in 1914. Five hundred pieces of English gold seemed to set a very serious seal on our mission.

Vrybov said, 'Your cover is that of clerks in the Foreign Office, currently employed in British embassies overseas. You must wear civilian clothing, not uniforms. If Stefan needs any you may buy them out of travel expenses. Be certain not to carry anything connected with the navy.'

'But supposing anyone questions us about the duties of clerks in the Foreign Office?'

'Tell them it's all confidential, of course.'

He handed me a card on which I read the the words 'Maxim Preobarski, 4 Irtysh IPProspekt, Tobolsk'. He said, 'This is your contact in Tobolsk. We understand the Romanovs live in the old Governor's Residence in Tobolsk and are allowed a certain amount of freedom, but always under guard. You and Stefan should learn this name and address and then destroy the card.'

He delved into an inside pocket and produced a brown envelope, addressed to me and marked, 'MOST SECRET'. It contained orders signed by Captain Blaze, instructing Stefan and me to proceed according to directions received from Count Vrybov. He said, 'You might need these in case of any future queries about your activities. Don't carry them with you — tuck them away somewhere safe at home.'

I thought his comment sounded a bit ominous but nodded obediently. He continued, 'You sail from Newcastle on the night after next, land in Norway thirty-six hours later and take the train to Sweden. Report to the British Embassy in Stockholm and they'll tell you how to go on to St Petersburg.'

He looked at me assessingly and asked, 'Any questions?'

'Shall we be armed? With pistols, maybe?'

16

'By no means! Diplomatic personnel don't carry weapons. Your story is that you're Foreign Office personnel given the task of helping British citizens who may still be in Russia, and experiencing difficulty because of the revolution.'

'I suppose we might even run into some of them.'

'Possibly, and perhaps you can help them. Even give them a few of your sovereigns. But your real mission is to make contact with the Emperor Nicholas and his family, advise them they would still be welcome in Britain, and do everything you can to help them and their supporters.'

'You really believe they can make a getaway?'

He grimaced as though that word was too lower-class to use for royalty, but said, 'Yes, with the help of local sympathizers. Your task is quite straightforward: to find a way to take the family down river to the north coast, supervise the journey by water, and take them to the Allied commander. Our forces will have landed at Murmansk and Archangel by that time, and will be able to take over from you and send the Romanovs on to Britain.'

He spoke with complete confidence, but a brief flash of memory reminded me that a senior officer had addressed us with similar confidence on the night before the disastrous landings at Gallipoli. But I said, 'I understand. And is there a letter, or something, to show the Emperor as proof of our mission?'

He tutted as though I was a stupid servant. 'Of course not. Suppose the Bolsheviks searched you, or your baggage, and came across it? You simply have to do what you're told.'

Automatically I said, 'Aye, aye, sir,' because that was the phrase we normally used to acknowledge orders. He looked at me as though he thought I was being sarcastic, then said very seriously, 'I have Captain Blaze's authority to tell you that, for important political reasons, everything about this mission must be kept absolutely secret until the results can be announced publicly.'

I said, 'I understand,' and he began to heave himself out of the car. He said, 'I must say goodbye to your mother,' and I took the briefcase and money-belts to my room. Mother was working in the garden as Vrybov walked towards her, and I returned just as she was waving him farewell. She said to me, 'Evgeni kept you talking for a long time. Did he have anything interesting to say?'

I wanted to tell her about it but remembered his injunction about secrecy. I answered, 'Not really. Just the usual war talk.'

She nodded, and turned back to her task of deadheading her roses.

4

We set out from Newcastle in the passenger-cargo ship *Toreador* on her regular run to Bergen in Norway: a long slant of 450 miles through waters that are usually cold and grey. There was a brisk wartime trade between Britain and neutral Norway, which the Germans tried equally briskly to destroy with surface ships and submarines. The *Toreador* was one of a convoy of ten ships escorted by four destroyers.

She carried only twelve passengers, all middle-aged businessmen and officials except for Stefan and me and Emery Porteous, a tall strong man with a round red face and a high-pitched nagging voice that dominated conversation in the ship's small dining saloon. He announced himself early as a correspondent for a London daily newspaper, and expressed blatant curiosity as to what Stefan and I, two obviously fit young men of fighting age, should be doing in civilian clothes on a ship bound for a neutral country.

We fobbed him off until the second day, when Stefan and I were sitting out on deck in fine clear weather. Porteous strayed up to us and tried to open a conversation but we were more interested in the evolutions of one of the destroyers, which was patrolling at some distance from the others. I saw it turn back towards the convoy and then its Aldis lamp began flashing a message to the escort commander. Unthinkingly, I read it out as, 'Possible enemy ships approaching south-east.'

Porteous demanded 'How can you read that?' so challengingly that I simply shrugged. Stefan said, 'Learnt it in the Boy Scouts, didn't he?'

A minute or so later the escort commander hoisted signals to the convoy to close up and increase speed, and I saw funnel smoke along the horizon. In the manner of fast-moving ships the newcomers seemed suddenly to jump into view. When I asked Stefan, 'What d'you make of them?', he said, 'Prob'ly a light cruiser and two destroyers,' just as the escort commander's siren began whooping and another string of signals fluttered up the halliards. The *Toreador*'s alarm bells rang and Porteous asked urgently, 'What's happening?'

I was too intent on watching the enemy to answer him. I saw the first flicker of gun flashes and counted the seconds until the first shells screeched overhead, sending up pillars of foam beyond the convoy. Our escort destroyers turned towards the enemy and I imagined their tactics: two to tackle the destroyers and two to make a torpedo attack on the light cruiser.

I saw the flash-flash-flash of gunfire and a forest of foam spouts leap out of the water between us and the enemy. Now it was a question of whether they would concentrate on our attacking escorts or seize the chance to blast some of the merchant ships. We passengers had been instructed that, in case of attack or other emergency, we should don our lifejackets and assemble in the smoke-room to await instructions. Stefan and I didn't give a thought to this and when one of the stewards came hurrying along, trying to round up the passengers in his care, Porteous also ignored him. To my surprise he pulled a notebook from his pocket and began jotting in it.

By that time the air was shuddering with the detonations of gunfire far and near. The *Toreador* carried a 4.7 inch quickfirer mounted on the stern and it crashed out two or three times, with its long spurts of flame and gush of yellow-brown smoke, when the gunner found targets. One of the merchant ships burst into flames that immediately raged fore and aft while another, engines stopped by a shell in the engineroom, drifted between the columns of the convoy.

Then one of our destroyers, racing along between us and the enemy, began laying a smokescreen which looked almost solid as rolls of black smoke bulged out of its funnels.

Firing slackened for a minute or so while all our escorts vanished through the smokescreen, then burst out again. Frustratingly, we could only guess at what was happening.

Then we heard a huge rumbling explosion from beyond the screen and I asked Stefan, 'What d'you make of that?'

'I reckon the Jerry cruiser copped a coupla torpedoes in her innards.'

Aggravated, Porteous cried out in his high-pitched voice, 'You two know all about this, don't you? Who the hell are you?'

I ignored him, listening to the sporadic firing which continued between the destroyers, but Stefan told him, 'We're just peaceful civil servants.'

The smokescreen drifted away while three of our destroyers steamed back towards us, their white bow-waves seeming to flaunt the cockiness of victory. The fourth followed after them, trailing smoke and steam but not seeming to be badly damaged.

Porteous made some more efforts to question us but we evaded them. Eventually he drifted away but he was in high fettle at dinner in the saloon that night, proclaiming his intention to write up the 'sea battle' for his newspaper if the censors allowed him to do so.

Then he proclaimed, 'In my opinion the Russian revolution is on its last legs. The Whites are hitting the Bolsheviks where it hurts. Mr Winston Churchill says the Bolshies must be defeated so Russia can start fighting the Germans again. That's why we're landing a force in northern Russia, to help bring the revolution to an end.'

He followed Stefan and me when we drifted into the smoke-room after dinner, and insisted on buying the drinks. Then he said, 'I suppose you chaps are going to Russia in connection with our troops landing in Murmansk?'

I asked, 'What makes you think we're going to Russia?'

He shrugged. 'The other passengers are businessmen bound for Norway and Sweden. You two look more like servicemen than commercial travellers and you obviously knew about ships fighting each other.'

Stefan said, 'I wish someone would invent a bloody big aeroplane to fly us where we're going, so we wouldn't have to sit around listening to arseholes like you.'

Unperturbed, Porteous said, 'I'm told that half a million tons of British war materials, delivered to Murmansk over the years, are simply lying there uselessly because of Russian inefficiency. We've certainly got to prevent the Bolshies getting hold of them.'

His know-all manner annoyed me so that I gulped my drink and stood up, saying, 'Long day tomorrow. Come along, Stefan.'

The long day started with the tedious formalities of landing at Bergen. I was annoyed by Porteous trying to catch a glimpse of our passports and I was about to say something when he yelped with pain. Stefan said, 'Oops, sorry, mate. Excuse my big feet.'

Two men met him and he drove off with them and I hoped we wouldn't see him again. But when we boarded the train to start our trip to Stockholm he was there on the platform, talking to four men of whom one was like a caricature German: corpulent, with rolls of fat on his thick neck and a head shaven to bristles, wearing a monocle and with duelling scars on his cheeks. I was close enough to hear them talking in a mixture of German and English.

On the train I encountered him in the restaurant car and asked him, 'Were those Germans you were talking to back there?'

24

'Yes, and they're on the train. They're journalists, like me. I knew a couple of them before the war.'

'For God's sake, man, you ought not to be chatting with bloody Jerries!'

He looked solemn. 'I told you, they're journalists. It's like an international brotherhood.'

I snorted 'Bullshit!' and pushed past him to a table.

In Stockholm, Stefan and I found the British Embassy crowded with Russian refugees hoping to be allowed to settle in Britain. But when I submitted our names we didn't have to wait long before being ushered into an inner office, where the official who received us wore the customary aloof expression of Foreign Office personnel in those days. He gave us tickets for a Swedish ship crossing the Baltic to St Petersburg on the following day and train tickets to Moscow. I asked, 'The trains are still running, then?' and he answered, 'If you're lucky.'

'Have you any instructions for us?'

'Report to the British Consulate-General in Moscow on arrival. Mr Bruce Lockhart is the man to see.'

'Do you know what conditions are like in Russia?'

'Chaotic, I believe. As you know, the

Bolsheviks made peace with the Germans but the German Army is still in Russia, and the Whites say they'll fight them as well as the Bolshies. The old Russian territories of Poland, Finland, Lithuania, Latvia and Estonia are fighting the Russkies for their own freedom. Escaped Czechoslovakian prisoners of war are joining up with the Whites.'

As we stood up to leave he said with sudden unexpected emotion, 'Ordinary people are going to suffer terribly.'

The ship for St Petersburg did not leave until the following morning and so we had time for a look at Stockholm. Stefan and I explored in leisurely fashion, had a few drinks and a couple of pleasant meals, and began strolling back to our hotel in that strange summer twilight of the northern latitudes when the sun merely dips below the horizon for a couple of hours. Some cafés and restaurants were still open and we were passing one of these when a bunch of men burst out of the doorway, yelling and struggling.

Stefan said, 'Hey — there's that newspaper bloke,' and I saw Porteous down on the pavement with some of them kicking him and bellowing insults in German. Four years earlier I'd been middleweight champion of the Home Fleet and Stefan was equally good with his fists and we waded into the conflict, for no good reason except for a dislike of seeing an Englishman beaten by a bunch of Jerries. We'd flattened a couple of them when a Swedish policeman came hurrying along. Everyone ignored him when he began bellowing orders in Swedish, but we took him more seriously when he drew the nasty-looking cutlass hanging from his belt.

The Germans tottered off with their black eyes and bleeding noses while Porteous stood dazed on the sidewalk with blood trickling from his scalp. But he recovered quickly and when I asked him, 'What the hell happened?' he said, 'We started arguing about the war and the Jerries lost their tempers.'

'So much for international brotherhood, eh?'

He grinned sheepishly. 'At least it's worth a try, I s'pose.'

5

Porteous attached himself to us as we boarded the ship for the 400-mile passage across the Baltic to St Petersburg. He had a romantic-looking bandage around his head and the German journalists, also on the ship, were adorned with sticking plaster. It could have been funny but we all ignored each other.

Few people were heading for St Petersburg but the docks there were crammed with refugees seeking a way out of Russia. There were no cabs or taxis but we noticed the Germans were met by a couple of uniformed German officers. Eventually we managed to push our way onto a streetcar and found our way to the railway station serving Moscow.

I'd visited St Petersburg as a boy, and remembered a city of fine buildings and noble prospects. But the buildings now all seemed to be neglected or damaged and the streets were littered and inhabited mainly by shabby unshaven soldiers and sailors with red stars in their caps.

Passengers for Moscow had to undergo rude questioning as to their reasons for travel and a lengthy examination of their papers, but Stefan and I were able to convince the officials we were attached to the British Consulate-General. Porteous's interrogation was concluded with the words, 'Be sure to tell the truth about our glorious revolution!'

After that we were allowed to pass through, but found the next train to Moscow would not leave for many hours. We were forbidden to leave the station in case we passed on our tickets to White sympathizers, and we found the station restaurant offered only cabbage soup, potatoes and weak tea.

Stefan and I were travelling very light but I found the weight of my money-belt a trifle irksome. In one of the filthy lavatory compartments, obviously uncleaned for months, I extracted five of the heavy little paper cylinders, of ten sovereigns apiece, and distributed them through my clothing.

When at last the Moscow train was announced we found it consisted only of four carriages, all showing the scars of war in their broken windows and tattered upholstery. There were not enough passengers to fill the carriages and when I remarked on this another man said, 'Everyone wants to get out of Moscow these days, not go there.'

The five German journalists turned up together with some German officers, all as raucous as though they were rulers of a conquered country. I was glad they weren't in our carriage.

The journey from St Petersburg to Moscow is only about the same length as that from London to Edinburgh but the rail track was in a sorry state and the train's speed varied erratically. After some hours we stopped at Bologje, where hungry passengers besieged the refreshment room but had to be satisfied with tea and a kind of wheaten porridge.

After that I dozed until I was awoken by screeching brakes together with shouting outside the train. A rough road ran alongside the permanent way and about twenty horsemen galloped along it followed by two men in an open car. Someone said, 'That'll be the Commissar of the local Soviet, wanting to inspect the passengers.'

I'd already learned that 'Commissar' meant 'official enforcing political principles' while 'Soviet' meant 'council of workers, soldiers and peasants'.

The horsemen dismounted and yelled for the passengers to climb down front the train, and when we did so they herded us into a field along the road. They'd taken rifles from the saddle holsters and looked ready to use them.

30

Passengers leaving the train included several men in the uniform of the new Red Army. One of them strode towards the two men in the car, shouting, 'Why the delay? We're late for duty in Moscow!'

The driver of the car, a youngish man in a plain khaki uniform, answered calmly, 'I'm Commissar Samatov of the Zamienski Soviet. It's my duty to inspect those entering our Soviet Area.'

'We were checked when we boarded the train! Enough of this nonsense!'

Samatov said, 'You think it's nonsense? Then discuss it with my colleague, Comrade Alieven of the Cheka.'

The dreaded word 'Cheka', an acronym for Russian words meaning extraordinary commission to fight counter-revolution and sabotage, pricked the Red Army man's balloon. He fell in with the rest of us but there were more passengers to come. The five German journalists descended unhurriedly from their carriage and wandered along the track, laughing and talking loudly in a manner which obviously derided the Russians.

Samatov watched them impassively until they joined the rest of us, and the riflemen pushed us all into line. Porteous muttered anxiously, 'What the hell's going on?' and I told him, 'Don't worry. The Russians never seem able to do anything without secret police pushing their noses in. The Cheka are simply the latest in a long line.'

Samatov and Alieven stepped out of the car to inspect us, moving slowly along the line and studying everyone's identity documents. Samatov had piercing grey-green eyes set in a pale bony face and Alieven was a middle-aged man with an expression of tolerant boredom. Samatov's eyes seemed to drill into mine when I gave him my diplomatic passport, which he scanned contemptuously and handed back with a mutter of 'Royalist!'

The Germans kept up their laughs and chatter while Samatov moved along the line, as though to show they cared nothing for Russian officialdom. He was frowning when he confronted them and he grew angrier when he rapped out questions in Russian and they answered in German. My knowledge of that language is fragmentary but when he asked one man, 'Why are you going to Moscow?', I understood the answer to be, 'Don't understand. Why don't you speak our language?', followed by a guffaw from the others.

One of them had carried a briefcase from the train and when Samatov demanded, 'Open that!', he clutched it protectively. Samatov snatched it from him, pulled it open and took out a sheaf of papers, which he scanned quickly before telling Alieven, 'Look! Some of these have Russian addresses! Why are Germans communicating with people in Moscow? Spies, they are! Capitalist spies!'

He ordered a couple of men to search the Germans, which they did thoroughly and roughly. He gave a cry of triumph when they found the corpulent man was carrying a Mauser Parabellum P.08 automatic in his attaché case together with some extra clips of 9 mm cartridges. The German babbled, 'It's only for self-protection — an army friend in St Petersburg lent it to me,' but the two Bolsheviks ignored him. For a couple of minutes they consulted in low voices and then Samatov shouted, 'These men are spies and would-be saboteurs and deserve no mercy! There's only one fate for those who would sabotage the revolution!'

He snapped orders to his men, who hustled the five Germans away from the rest of us and pushed them into line. The Germans may not have understood Russian but they understood the way a dozen or so men began to form a firing squad. Their horrified faces stared at the riflemen and then at the rest of us, who stood there as though paralysed but equally horrified by what was about to happen. I heard Porteous gasp, 'Jesus! Jesus!'

I've never known what made me step towards Samatov. I suppose it was because the navy had trained me to deal justly with everyone and the firing squad certainly would not do that. I said politely, 'I have a proposal for you, comrade. I would like to buy your prisoners.'

He scoffed, 'Are you crazy? Do you think we are capitalists, buying and selling human beings?'

He half-turned to the firing squad, mouth open on the final orders, but Alieven said calmly, 'Wait,' and asked me, 'What are you offering for the prisoners?'

'Five golden English sovereigns apiece.'

'Show me.'

I gave him one of the cylindrical packets of sovereigns and he broke it open. The coins clinked musically on his palm, glistening with the special lustre of gold. There's something about gold which is hypnotically different from other coinage, or paper money, and the two men stared at it as I said gently, 'I'm sure twenty-five sovereigns will be of great assistance to your Soviet.'

I expected Alieven to ask where I got the money, and why I wanted to help the Germans. But he simply held out his hand and said, 'Thirty.'

I felt the moment wasn't ripe for

bargaining and gave him the money. He muttered, 'Let's go,' to Samatov and within a minute or so the horsemen were trotting away with the two officials following in their car.

The corpulent German was in a state of semi-collapse. Two of his friends helped him back to the train, while another of them came across to me and gave the stiff little nod and bow with which Germans introduce themselves. He barked, 'I am Theodor Pfalz. My colleagues and I . . . speak little English . . . but we express — ah — devoted gratitude.'

I nodded acceptance and said, 'Do me a favour, then. Promise not to report this incident in your newspapers. Understood?'

He gave me another stiff little bow and said, 'Agreed. With deepest gratitude.'

I was beginning to wonder how I'd account for the expenditure when Porteous gloated, 'Gee whiz! What a story!'

I told him, 'Forget it. I can guarantee the censor won't pass it. And just to make sure I'll ask the British Consul in Moscow to pass the word on to London.'

I'd no idea whether that could be done but Porteous didn't know either. He complained, 'Always the bloody same. Whenever I get a scoop someone buggers it up.'

He trudged back to the train and I was

about to follow him when Stefan said, 'How about this, then?'

He bent and scooped up the pistol and cartridges, half-hidden in the grass where Samatov had flung them down and then forgotten them. I said, 'Bring them along. They might come in handy.'

6

We bade farewell to Porteous in Moscow, where the journalist he was relieving said, 'Thank God I'm getting out of this bloody place!' After that we went to the British Consular-General, who greeted us with, 'Oh yes, I'm instructed to help you get to Tobolsk. I won't ask why you're going there because everyone in Russia knows the Romanovs have been there since last August.'

He pulled items from a drawer while he told me, 'I should advise you that Nicholas Romanov is a weak-willed nonentity married to an hysterical neurotic bitch. Of course the basic problem is that Russian royalty believes it has the divine right to do whatever it pleases, without accepting advice from anyone. That's why Nicholas, together with the rest of his family and the Russian aristocracy, made such an appalling balls-up of the war against Germany.'

I was accustomed to senior officers ranting about everything that displeased them and so I simply enquired, 'How far is it to Tobolsk?'

'Well over a thousand miles, and you'll be bloody lucky to get there! God knows what condition the railways are in!'

He handed me an envelope, saying, 'Here's your tickets, plus identification papers certifying you're attached to this office.' Next came two packets of Russian banknotes, with the commentary, 'I can't guarantee how long this will retain its value but at least it will buy you a few cups of tea.'

Finally he handed over a letter typed in both English and Russian, saying, 'We used to have a consular agency in Omsk, which is where you leave the train and go downriver to Tobolsk, and this letter says you're studying possible suitable locations for a consulate in western Siberia. I don't know whether it will convince the Cheka but it does give you a reason for travel.'

I thanked him for everything and asked, 'Do you think the revolution will succeed?'

He nodded emphatically. 'Yes, because the Bolshies are so bloody ruthless. They won't stop at anything to get their way and they're promising so much to the workers and peasants — though God knows if they'll keep their promises.'

We went from his office to the Yaroslavl Station, where the Trans-Siberian Express began its 6000-mile journey to the Pacific coast. We had to wait two uncomfortable days for seats in an overcrowded train, which ground its way slowly eastwards. Sometimes it jolted slowly along the worn-out track, sometimes it sat motionless in sidings while troop trains rattled past, and quite often it simply waited at stations for reasons not revealed to passengers. Fortunately it was fine summer weather. There was nothing to eat on the train and most of the station restaurants were closed but peasant women sold us food at stops along the way.

On one such occasion, when we were negotiating for black bread and sausage, we met Dr Eugene Stasanowski. He was a small taut man in his forties, wearing a shabby uniform from which the rank badges and decorations had been stripped. Standing next to me as we bought our dinners he said, 'You speak very good Russian but your accent is unfamiliar to me.'

I told him I was English and he nodded without comment. We chatted a bit as the train trundled on and he told me that he and his field hospital had been captured by the Germans a year or so earlier, and released after the peace treaty had been signed. He said, 'I was lucky the Bolsheviks only cut off my shoulder-straps and decorations. They spared me because I am a doctor but shot the other officers in my unit.'

He was making his way home to

Ekaterinburg in the Ural Mountains, and he left the train at a junction next morning. Of course, I couldn't guess at how much he was going to mean to us.

A couple of countrymen squeezed into his vacant seat. They were sharing a bottle of vodka and already well sozzled, singing and talking loudly. One asked the other, 'Did you see the Emperor in Tobolsk during the winter?'

'Aye, and all his family, walking to church in the snow. There were only a couple of recruits to guard them and they could have walked on to China if they wanted.'

'Where were they living then?'

'Some old wreck of a house called the governor's mansion. The Eastern Urals Soviet fixed it up for them but — '

Of course I was listening eagerly but another passenger shouted, 'Shut up about the cursed Emperor! Who cares about him and his swinish family!'

Next day we reached Omsk, an unattractive city swept by duststorms and crammed with refugees and Red Army soldiers. I expected to be checked and questioned by the local Soviet but nobody took any notice of us when we went, with many others, to buy tickets on one of the paddle steamers plying the River Irtysh.

After a couple of days we reached Tobolsk, sprawling along high riverbanks crowned by an old fortress. I had the pleasant feeling that the long lead-in to our mission was at last going to seem worthwhile and as soon as we landed I asked the way to the address of our contact in Tobolsk.

After a long trudge we found the street and walked along it for a little way, and came to an abrupt halt when we saw the door of No. 4 had been smashed in. Some of the windows were broken, with the marks of fire and smoke above one of them, and there were a few bullet holes in the walls.

We stopped and stared a little too long, because a Red Army man spotted us from inside the house and came bustling out to check on us. When he saw we were obvious strangers, carrying backpacks, he yelled for support and two more men came out to join him. 'Papers!' he snapped, and held out a grubby hand.

When he'd examined them, including the letter from the Consulate-General, he growled, 'But what do you want here?'

I'd had enough time to think up a story and I said, 'Just lost our way, that's all. We're looking for somewhere to stay and must have taken a wrong turning.'

He received that with a suspicious stare,

but shoved the papers back at us and said, 'Be on your way, then.'

I took my time about returning my papers to an inside pocket, and asked as though casually, 'Is it true the Romanov family lives here in Tobolsk?'

'What business is that of yours?'

I shrugged. 'None. Just curious, that's all.'

'Well, they were here for a few months but they've been moved to Ekaterinburg. Take my advice and don't ask questions about them — the Cheka don't like it!'

7

We walked away as briskly as possible without seeming to hurry, and after a couple of minutes Stefan asked, 'What d'you think, then?'

I told him, 'Pretty obvious, isn't it? The royalists must've got a bit too big for their boots, and the Reds jumped on them.'

'D'you think that's why the Romanovs have been moved?'

'Can't say. Don't know what happened first.'

'So what shall we do?'

'Find somewhere we can stay while we work it out.'

Some forms of private enterprise seemed to be surviving and we found a room in a scruffy little inn. It was there, overhearing scraps of conversation, we learned the White Army's summer offensive was having some success. They were moving towards Tobolsk, and that may have been the real reason why the Romanovs had been transferred to Ekaterinburg.

It occurred to me that, if we waited a while, the Whites would roll back the Reds and liberate the imperial family. That would give me an excuse to abandon our mission and make for the Allied forces in northern Russia.

But that wasn't the way of the Royal Navy. Training, inheritance and instinct compelled me to keep trying. I didn't want to retrace our steps through Omsk, and with some careful questions I found the nearest route to Ekaterinburg was by horse or foot through the long broad range of hills known as the Ural Mountains. The distance was about 400 miles but with any luck we might be able to board a train at the railhead at Tiumen.

We found the equivalent of an English livery stable but the owner was wary of hiring horses to us. Horses were in short supply because the Red Army had commandeered so many of them. When I asked if he would sell us the horses, for English sovereigns, he would only say, 'Show me.'

We were in his cluttered little office, where there was hardly room for the three of us plus his head groom, Andrei Pyrudin. This individual, a man of middle age, smelt pungently of sweat and urine, both horse and human, and had hidden most of his face behind a thicket of grey-brown whiskers. A pair of cunning little eyes watched me open one of the cylinders of sovereigns.

Eventually the owner agreed to hire out a

couple of horses on condition Pyrudin rode with us, showed us the way and brought the horses back to Tobolsk. That suited me and I wanted to leave immediately, but the owner wouldn't have that and told us to return next morning. At least that gave Stefan and me the time to buy some ill-fitting second-hand riding gear, but when we returned next morning the owner growled, 'Andrei's sick. Come back tomorrow.'

I suspected the owner of some kind of trick but when we returned next morning our mounts were ready. They were Siberian ponies, sturdy and nimble. Stefan and I hadn't done much riding since our country childhoods but we managed to stay on.

The Urals are not really mountains but a complex of high steep hills, often thickly forested, rich in minerals and with many active or abandoned mine workings. Pyrudin led us along earthen roads winding through the hills, passing occasional farms or villages, and my spirits rose as we trotted along. We covered about twenty miles before we paused to water the horses and eat some of the food we'd brought with us.

After that Pyrudin led us along a lonely stretch where dense pine forests rose on either side. I suspected something when he began to ride more slowly, until we heard hoofbeats behind us and he exclaimed, 'Robbers! Quick — follow me!'

I didn't think quickly enough to object when he turned off the track into a steep-sided gully, which I hoped might be some kind of short cut to safety. But the gully ended abruptly in the entrance to an abandoned mine, where a pair of rusty rails ran into the dark mouth. Our ponies bumped together as I asked Pyrudin, 'Where have you brought us, idiot?'

His yellow teeth grinned through his whiskers and I suddenly understood why he'd taken a day off. I'd thought his 'sickness' was only an overdose of vodka but obviously he'd spent the time in contacting accomplices. Three riders in shabby, unkempt uniforms, with carbines in their saddle holsters, galloped up the gully after us and I guessed they were deserters from one army or another.

I tried to put a brave face on it by demanding, 'Who are you? What do you want?', and their leader touched his cap in mock humility. 'Only your horses, your honour. And those bags you're carrying. And the gold coins we're told you have in your pocket.'

His accomplices guffawed at this and edged their horses closer, until the six of us were pressed closely together in front of the mine entrance. It looked like a dark mouth waiting to consume a couple of us.

The leader suddenly stopped grinning and snapped, 'Don't waste our time, then. Hand over your money!'

Stefan said, 'Here — have mine.'

His right hand delved inside his jacket and I felt a spurt of angry astonishment that he should give in so easily. I'd almost forgotten the German pistol tucked into his waistband, though I'd seen him inspecting and handling it occasionally when we were on our own. It was a deadly efficient piece of machinery with its four-inch barrel, checkered butt, and trigger and trigger-guard neatly integrated into the body of the piece. He seemed to enjoy playing with the weapon but I'd never had much interest in handguns.

He cocked the pistol and clicked off the safety-catch as he pulled the pistol out of his jacket. The robber tried to grab the muzzle but he was too slow. Stefan fired and the bullet blasted a horrible mass of blood, bone and brains out of the robber's skull.

The shot caused the horses to rear wildly, so that the corpse toppled across another of the robber's mounts. This obstructed him as he tried to pull his carbine out of the saddle holster, but perhaps gave him enough time to

47

wonder why he and his collaborators had attempted a hold-up without weapons in their hands. Possibly Pyrudin had told them we were unarmed.

Stefan shot the second man neatly through the chest, then turned his pistol on the sole survivor. This one screamed 'No! No!' as he tried to drag his horse around but Stefan shot him twice in the body. The horse bolted as he fell off, one foot caught in a stirrup, and the body bounced wildly behind the horse as it galloped away.

Stefan's ruddy face had turned a dirty grey-green. He leaned over to vomit his recent lunch and gasped, 'Jesus! I never killed anyone up close before! Bit different from ships shooting at each other, isn't it?'

He turned towards Pyrudin, who was wailing and blubbering as he covered his whiskery face with his hands, and raised the pistol again. I yelled, 'No, don't!', but he asked, 'Why not? He must have set those bastards on to us, right? Sir?'

'Because his boss will probably expect him back, together with the horses. If he doesn't turn up we'll be suspected.'

'Oh, I dunno. I doubt anyone'd worry about him.'

'Do as you're bloody well told.'

'Yessir.'

He leaned over and grabbed Pyrudin's whiskers, snapping, 'Hey, old pig's bladder! You got a drink?'

Pyrudin extracted a smeared bottle from a saddle-bag and Stefan washed out his mouth with the vodka and then took a hefty drink. Pyrudin's sly little eyes watched us as we talked in English, discussing our next move. After some pros and cons we decided to throw the deserters' bodies into the mine entrance but keep their horses and equipment. Their horses were bigger than the ponies and would be easier for us to ride. If anyone asked questions about them we'd say we found them wandering. If possible we'd catch the horse which bolted and free it from the body.

Pyrudin worked with us as we disposed of the bodies and then stood watching us submissively. By that time I'd realized that if we let him go he'd return to Tobolsk and he'd probably betray us. But if we took him along with us to Tiumen he might betray us to Bolsheviks met on the way.

Stefan and I exchanged a few muttered words as we worked and when we'd finished he asked, 'So what d'you think? Changed your mind?'

I shrugged. 'Up to you.'

'Does that mean I'm the official murderer for this crew?'

'I didn't mean it like that.'

'But it's what you're thinking, isn't it?'

Very slowly he drew the Mauser out again. He held it loosely, moistening his lips, then muttered, 'Oh shit, I can't do it. Anyway, how'd we find the way to Tiumen without him to guide us?'

I thought we'd probably work it out somehow, but Stefan turned to Pyrudin and asked, 'Listen, old cunt whiskers, you want to live?'

Pyrudin nodded vigorously, his eyes glistening with unusual sincerity.

Stefan said, 'Right, then. You can take us to Tiumen, but any tricks will earn you a bullet. Understood?'

Pyrudin nodded again and Stefan gestured for him to mount. We rode down the gully and on to the main track, keeping an eye out for the horse that had bolted but not seeing it again. I hoped someone might find it and relieve it of the burden of the dead body, thinking that to be just another symptom of the revolution.

Late in the day we came to a farmhouse whose occupants were suspicious at first but, shown a couple of sovereigns, put us up for the night and let us put our mounts in the steep paddock close to the house. Pyrudin seemed subdued and grateful and I was foolish enough to think I could trust him. Next morning, of course, we found he had gone and taken the ponies with him — but at least he'd left the cavalry horses behind.

Stefan said, 'The old bastard'll probably set the Bolshies after us,' but I sensed he wouldn't want to reveal what he'd been up to. We heard no more about him and so I may have been right.

We set off again on the track to Tiumen and soon caught up with some other travellers going the same way, and amenable to us joining them. If they noticed we rode horses with army brands and equipment they asked no questions about them or about our reasons for travel, which was no more than tactful in those days.

In Tiumen we had the good fortune to find a train was leaving for Ekaterinburg within a few hours. The Red Army was in charge of the station but did no more than grumble about 'foreign capitalists' before allowing us to buy tickets. As for the horses, nobody seemed to notice when we simply turned them into a paddock in the goods yard where numerous other horses, of various types and sizes, awaited Bolshevik selection.

8

We found Ekaterinburg to be a handsome little city with broad streets and some fine buildings, the centre of a rich mining area where, for a couple of centuries, men had tunnelled the hills in search of gold, platinum and other precious minerals. It was also a rail centre for the Urals and a market for Siberian produce, and an important communist centre for western Siberia.

When our slow train from Tiumen pulled into Ekaterinburg station, we found it was thronged with Red Army men, civilians seeing them off, and 'agitprop' units pumping out propaganda to strengthen the soldiers' resolution. Obviously they were bound for the Omsk front, then threatened by the White Army.

Stefan and I were pushing through the crowd when something about us attracted the attention of a couple of men in workmen's garb, with red stars in their caps and pistol-belts round their waists They shoved their way towards us and demanded, 'Papers!'

The letter from the Consulate-General, and our diplomatic passports, failed to impress them. Perhaps it was because we'd been unable to shave for a few days, and our stubbled features didn't resemble the photographs, or perhaps they simply couldn't read. They muttered together and I caught the word 'spion', and said loudly, 'We are British representatives, not spies!'

One of them said sneeringly, 'You'd better come and explain yourselves, then!', and they pushed us through the crowds to what had been the stationmaster's office. Two men sat in it behind a table heaped with papers, and one of them snapped, 'What do you want? We're trying to despatch five regiments today!'

One of our captors answered, 'Beg pardon, comrades, but there's something suspicious about these two men.'

He handed over our papers and the one who had spoken glanced through them, then asked, 'Who authorized you to come to Ekaterinburg?'

The arrogance in his tone triggered a similar response from me. I said, 'Who are you be to be asking that?'

He scanned me for a few moments but then answered quite mildly, 'I am Commissar Goloschekin of the Ekaterinburg Soviet and this is Comrade Beloborodov of the Cheka.'

I answered, 'Our instructions, as you can

see in that letter I showed you, are to seek a suitable place for a British consular agency in Siberia. We understand your government, in Moscow, agreed to this. Nobody told us to seek further permission.'

Beloborodov snapped, 'Then they should have done! Your passports say you are subjects of 'His Britannic Majesty', and everyone knows that Nicholas Romanov and his family are here in Ekaterinburg and that he's related to your so-called King-Emperor! There's something suspicious about two British officials coming here!'

I tended to agree with him, but asked, 'Why should there be? The British government has already refused asylum to the Romanovs.'

Goloschekin said, 'Enough of this arguing,' and nodded to the men who had arrested us. He ordered, 'Search them.'

In modern parlance, that made me blow my top. In a voice accustomed to giving orders over the sounds of wind and sea I shouted, 'I represent King George the Fifth of Great Britain! My colleague and I refuse to submit to the indignity of searches! If you do so it must be by force and you may kill us as you do — and then try to explain yourselves to the government of Britain!'

Stefan chimed in with, 'I agree!'

Of course all this sounds ludicrous nowadays but it did not in 1918. The British Empire ruled over a fifth of the world's population, with enormously important trade and cultural connections. Despite huge losses in the First World War, the British armed forces were still massively powerful.

The Bolshevik officials stared at me with a mixture of amusement and astonishment, until Beloborodov said drily, 'Well, no need for dramatics. We'll accept that you're here in good faith but don't give us cause for suspicion. Otherwise you'll find your government is a long way away.'

He handed our papers back to us and the two guards shoved us out of the room, obviously disappointed they weren't going to beat us up. Stefan kept close behind me as we pushed our way out of the station. He said, 'That was a close one. If they'd searched us they'd have found the Mauser and all that money.'

We emerged into the usual crowd which besieged railway stations in wartime: beggars, hawkers, pickpockets, homeless children, would-be passengers, prostitutes, families seeing off conscripts, and so on. I looked in vain for a cab or taxi and a boy of about twelve dodged towards us, offering, 'Carry your bags, comrades.'

He was ragged, dirty and hungry-looking, with the look of combined cunning and despair common to the orphans created by war and revolution. We shook our heads to his offer but I said, 'You can show us to a hotel, though.'

He said, 'The American hotel's the best. The foreign mining engineers used to stay there.'

'All right. Show us the way.'

He grinned with sudden boyish mischief. 'But the Cheka has taken it over for their headquarters. What about Bykov's hotel?'

'Let's have a look at it.'

He guided us through the crowds, asking, 'You're foreigners, aren't you? What are you — engineers? Ekaterinburg's full of strangers and foreigners these days. Even the Romanovs, did you know that?'

I didn't want to display any interest but asked, 'What are you, then? A stranger or a foreigner?'

'My family came from the village of Schuskenaya, but my father was killed in the war. My mother brought me and my two sisters here, looking for work, but she got sick and died. A family took my sisters in but they didn't want me.'

Stefan asked, 'What's your name?'

'Sasha, which is short for Aleksandr. Would

you like to see where the Romanovs live? It's along that way.'

'All right.'

'You'll pay me, then? I have to make a living.'

'All right.'

He led us along a side street, and we had to trudge for some distance until we reached the huts and cottages on the outskirts of town. Sasha told us, 'The Soviet took a rich merchant's house to put the Romanovs in. He made a big fuss but everyone laughed and said it served him right for being rich.'

When we came to the house we found it stood on a large block of land at the junction of two streets, not far from the edge of the forest-lands surrounding the town. A high wooden palisade, of boards of irregular length, had been thrown up between the house and the streets. At one point I glimpsed the movement of a bayoneted rifle where a sentry walked his beat.

Sasha said, 'When the family first came here people would crowd around to have a look at them, but the Cheka always keep them inside the house. Nobody bothers much nowadays.'

The house was a sizeable brick mansion of about twenty rooms. From where we stood we could see only the upper storey above the palisade. The windows had been white-washed, obviously to prevent the prisoners from signalling to anyone outside. I felt a pang of sympathy for anyone kept under such claustrophobic conditions.

I was wary of attracting attention by standing and staring and so I kept us walking until we'd gone a little way into the forest. Rough tracks, made by horsedrawn vehicles, ran amongst the trees. Many of these had been felled for firewood or building.

I said something about the vandalized appearance of the area and Sasha said, 'It's even worse further on. All kinds of old mine workings, with rusty machinery and rubbish everywhere.'

I thought we'd dallied around long enough and we tramped back into town, where Sasha guided us to Bykov's hotel. I gave him some money and he said briskly, 'I'll work for you while you're here, right? I'll be outside when you need me.'

I didn't ask where he slept or how he lived, feeling I'd prefer not to know.

The hotel fed us more or less adequately and we picked up rumours in the bar. Of course there was no radio or TV in those days and most Russian newspapers had ceased publication but everyone passed on rumours or gossip. The feeling was that the Whites were pushing the Reds back and that they'd soon assault Ekaterinburg to rescue the Romanovs. Stefan asked me, 'What if the Whites do break through? Could they rescue Nicholas?'

I'd been wondering the same thing and I said, 'Probably the Reds would move him and the family out before then.'

He thought that over, then asked, 'Do you think there's any hope of getting them out of that place they're in?'

I'd been trying to prevent my thoughts from moving along the same lines. It seemed impossible for the two of us to get into the house and emerge with Nicholas and his family. And if there were any White sympathizers in the town I'd no idea how to find or approach them. Everything looked very different from the way Captain Blaze and Count Vrybov had laid it out for me in England.

But my training forbade me to show doubts or despondency, or even to accept the logical option of waiting to see whether the Whites would capture Ekaterinburg. I'd been given a job to do and it was my duty to do it . . . or attempt to do so, anyway.

I told Stefan briskly, 'We'll have a good walk around town tomorrow. See what we can find out.'

Sasha was happy to escort us and we let him act as our guide — though it was hard to tell him what we were looking for. But we did see a roughly painted board outside one of the houses, announcing Dr E. Stasanowski's consulting hours. I told Stefan we'd met Stasanowski on the train and he said, 'He's already very popular. He charges poor people only what they can pay or give him — sometimes nothing. The Bolsheviks say all medical treatment will be free but it hasn't happened yet.'

We saw queues waiting outside shops, hoping to buy food, and marching units of the Red Army, and armed men wearing red stars who watched everyone suspiciously, and hurrying people who did not meet one's eyes. Whites? Or Reds? Or simply ordinary folk hoping to survive?

Almost inevitably our wanderings led us back to the house which held the Romanovs. Nothing had changed except that a battered Fiat motor lorry now stood outside the front entrance. Its driver was chatting to one of the armed guards, and they glanced at us but took no particular notice. I had a sudden wild notion of presenting myself at the gate and, on the excuse I was looking for premises for a British consular agency, asking to examine the house.

But we strolled on and I offered Stefan a *papyrossi*, the cigarette of which about half the length consists of a cardboard tube. Sasha also held out his hand for one, and puffed away like a veteran smoker. I said idly, 'I wonder how many people are in the Romanov party?', and Sasha answered, 'Eleven.'

Stefan scoffed, 'How do you know that?'

'Everyone knows. There are Nicholas and Alexandra, their five children, a doctor, a cook and two servants. Anyway, I know Pyotr Orloff, the kitchen boy who works for the Cheka guard and their cook. He's from my village.'

He took a final puff at the *papyrossi* and flicked the cardboard tube away, asking, 'Why are you interested in the Romanovs?'

'Just curiosity.'

'I think it's more than that. You're foreigners, you've been here twice, and you ask questions about them.'

I looked into his sharp young face and he gave me his cheeky grin, with its edge of desperation. He said, 'I bet you're American newspaper men. There was one in Ekaterinburg a few weeks ago but the Cheka chased him away. Anyway, I'm hungry. Give me a few roubles and I won't tell the Cheka about you.'

His eyes glistened when I peeled some notes off the roll that was losing value every day, and put them in his grubby hand. He winked and trotted away. Stefan and I strolled after him, and I remembered the Romanov family as I'd met them on the beach in that faraway summer. I wondered how such a family felt, once worshipped as semi-divine, now they were shut away in that house on the edge of nowhere. I said something about that to Stefan, who said, 'And I bet the Reds will hang on to them. Use them as hostages.'

We walked back into town, where we found a certain amount of excitement because of the arrival of an agitprop train. Armed guards were rounding up an audience for frenzied political speeches and playlets and we were pushed in with the others.

Suddenly Sasha was there again, nibbling a cold baked potato. He ate slowly, jacket and all, in the manner of people who don't know when there'll be any more. When he'd finished he said, 'That's Iakov Iurovsky talking now,' and pointed to the makeshift platform where a man was giving one of the speeches.

Stefan asked, 'Who's he?'

'The Cheka man in charge of the Romanovs.'

He was a youngish man, in shabby ordinary clothes and a peaked cap, but his face had a kind of fanatical intensity that lent conviction to what he had to say. I almost believed him.

When the show was over we were glad of the scrappy meal at the hotel, consisting mainly of greasy cabbage soup. We'd just finished when, through a dining-room window, I saw Sasha staring intently at the hotel. I guessed he wanted me and went outside, and with an air of great secrecy he beckoned to me to follow him round the corner. There he said, 'You know Pyotr Orloff I told you about? I saw him just now, sent into town to buy something. He told me the Romanovs are to be moved away tonight.'

I wondered if this was a ploy to cajole a few more roubles out of me, and asked, 'Can I speak to Pyotr, then?'

'No, he's gone back to the house. But he told me he heard some of Comrade Iurovsky's men talking.'

'So what did he hear them say?'

'He reckons that one of the guards said: 'Not much sleep tonight. Comrade Iurovsky wants Nicholas and his gang sent on their way after sunset.''

9

In those latitudes sunset is around midnight, when the sun dips below the horizon for a couple of hours. We arrived at the house when the light was growing dim and we could see a blur of lights behind the whitewashed windows, but it was still light enough outside for us to see the Fiat lorry had been moved to the front door of the house.

I wasn't sure why I wanted to watch the Romanovs being taken away. Stefan and I couldn't prevent it from happening. I simply felt it was my duty to be there, and follow them if possible and try to find where they would be taken next.

We'd checked out of the hotel and we were carrying our backpacks in case there was any chance of following. As for Sasha, he had tagged along uninvited.

I wondered if the Romanov party would have to walk to the railway station, with the lorry carrying their baggage. There was no sign of any other transport.

Standing under some trees across the road from the house we saw the upper storey of the house darken as activity moved downstairs, but anything happening on the ground floor was hidden from us by the palisade. For some minutes everything was quiet. Other houses in the street, scattered down the hill, were all in darkness because gas and electricity supplies were erratic and lamp oil unobtainable by civilians.

I began to wonder if young Pyotr's information had been based on guesswork. Then we heard a muffled voice, raised as though making some kind of declaration, followed instantly by a shot.

That triggered off women's screams, male voices shouting, and an irregular fusillade of shots. All the sounds were dulled because they happened inside the house, but I had a wild thought that some sort of rescue attempt was going on. That faded when Stefan groaned, 'Christ — they're killing them!'

The shooting stopped but we heard more screams, and men shouting confusedly. Long afterwards I heard they followed the shots with bayonets and rifle-butts.

Nothing could have stopped me from running across the road, to peer through a gap between boards in the palisade. I saw a couple of men holding lanterns and looking in the front door, just as the yelling inside the house rose to a crescendo. Then three or four men, dragging a body between them, crowded out of the door. One of them yelled, 'Hey, you'd never believe it! The old bitch and the girls have jewels sewn inside their corsets! Some of the bullets just bounced off of them!'

Other men, also dragging bodies, tumbled out of the door. They were all yelling in ferocious excitement and I actually heard some hideous laughter. One yelled, 'Look — diamonds! Help yourself!'

Then Iurovsky burst out of the door and fired his pistol in the air, shouting, 'I'll kill any swine stealing jewels! They now belong to the Party! Get those bodies on the lorry! Move! Move!'

Obviously the Cheka had killed the doctor and servants as well as the Romanovs, because there were more than six bodies. When all the corpses had been bundled into the lorry tray there was some shouting about 'Not enough room for everyone to ride!' which was obvious because there were about a dozen murderers plus Iurovsky and the lorry driver.

Iurovsky stopped the argument by ordering those who could not find space on the tray to run along behind, while he climbed in with the driver. When the engine started we crouched down behind the palisade until the lorry chugged out of the gate and turned on to the road through the forest.

Obviously the lorry had seen hard wartime service. It had solid rubber tyres, its engine coughed and wheezed asthmatically and the steering seemed erratic. Laden with the eleven bodies, plus as many of the murderers as had been able to climb aboard, it panted and lurched along the switchback road in the light of its oil-burning headlights, proceeding so slowly that the men unable to cram themselves in the tray had no trouble in running behind.

A strange mixture of emotions kept me trotting along the rough road, with Stefan and Sasha gasping behind me. Absurdly, I wanted revenge. The royal couple meant nothing to me but I was disgusted by the savage murder of their children and servants. My sense of duty impelled me to follow through: to see if, even now, there was something I could do. And I had a simple wish to see what would happen next. I spared a thought for young Sasha, feeling I should tell him to buzz off, but he probably wouldn't have obeyed me.

The lorry travelled about three miles before it turned off the road into a clearing which had been a mine site. A party of about thirty men, carrying candle lanterns or hurricane lamps, cheered the party's arrival. They were all more or less drunk and they stumbled towards the lorry crying out such things as, 'Hoorah for the Western Urals Soviet . . . Hand over the cursed Romanovs . . . I've sharpened my knife to cut their throats . . . '

As we moved cautiously after the last of the Cheka stragglers who had followed the lorry, I could see the mine site was still scattered with rusty pieces of machinery, a tangle of wire ropes, rotten timbers, and bricks torn from the circular wall around the top of the mineshaft. Forest grew thickly around the clearing and we had no difficulty in dodging into cover.

The rabble of Bolsheviks welcoming the lorry seemed to be civilians rather than soldiers but it was hard to see them clearly as they reeled around singing fragments of revolutionary songs and offering their bottles to the Cheka men. Iurovsky saw things were getting out of hand and bawled for silence, then shouted, 'Comrades, we've brought you the Romanovs but you won't have the pleasure of disposing of them. We unearthed a White plot to rescue them and — '

A howl of angry disappointment cut him short, plus yells of 'You promised them to us!' Then one of the Cheka men shouted, 'Wait till you see their jewels, comrades! They've got jewels hidden on their bodies worth millions of roubles!'

The drunks changed their tune, bawling, 'Hand them over, then! Let's have our share!' until Iurovsky fired over their heads and shouted, 'Any jewellery belongs to the Party and the People! I'll bring firing squads to deal with any thievery!'

That quietened them down and they listened to him demand that the bodies should be stripped and burned and the remnants thrown down the mine shaft. 'There must be nothing left for the Whites to find and preserve as icons!'

By that time Stefan and Sasha and I were almost mingling with his listeners. The sky was beginning to lighten but it was still shadowy under the trees and I suppose that, if any of the Western Urals Soviet gang glimpsed us, they thought we belonged to the Cheka, and vice versa.

Iurovsky had impressed them with his speech and, drunk as most of them were, they began to obey his orders. Men on the lorry dumped the first body on the ground, others began to search it for jewels, and a large group collected wood to build the fire. Within a couple of minutes the first flames began to crackle.

Suddenly I determined to salvage something out of the disaster. Even if we could rescue one body, and hide it somewhere until the advancing Whites could deal with it, and perhaps use the grave as a shrine, it would be a minor triumph. And something, at least, to report to Captain Blaze and the count, rather than total failure.

I whispered a few words to Stefan to tell him what I had in mind, then murmured, 'Let's see if we can grab the next body and carry it into the trees.'

Good sailor that he was, he nodded without question. I muttered to Sasha, 'Look after our backpacks until we come back.'

Our plain clothes had had rough enough treatment over the past few weeks to blend in with those of working-class Russians. I waited for a good moment to move forward and it came when the firemakers heaped some dry pine branches on the blaze. They exploded into an eruption of crackling sparks, pouring upwards and distracting attention.

Stefan and I dodged forward just as the two men on the lorry dumped another corpse on to the ground, and two of those waiting there dragged it towards the fire. Half a dozen more waited their turn but they'd just begun to pass round another bottle of vodka, and nobody in the boozy sweating bunch objected when Stefan and I moved through them to pick up the next corpse thrown off the lorry.

The clothing, and what was inside it, told me we were carrying a female. I felt a spasm of disgust as my fingers encountered a stiff sticky mass of fabric soaked in blood, but quelled it as we moved first towards the fire and then veered towards the shelter of the trees. Just as we did so someone threw more wood on the fire and a great tongue of flame licked upwards, causing us to pause in fear of discovery. But those around the fire all faced towards it, either feeding the flames or kneeling over the corpses in search of jewels and yelling exultantly when they found any. I glimpsed Iurovsky watching this work and gulped, 'Come on.'

We bundled the body into the shadows round the clearing and then into the deeper shelter of the forest. Sasha had been watching our efforts and he quickly joined us. Stefan and I were gasping and stumbling with the effort as we blundered through the forest until we could only just hear the Bolsheviks and glimpse the torrent of sparks pouring upwards. When Stefan tripped and fell I almost collapsed, with the body between us. I sat with my back against a tree trunk, my heart pounding as I wondered what I'd got myself into. Suppose the body wasn't even one of the Romanovs, but a servant? Even if it was a Romanov, what would we do with it until we contacted the Whites? Would they even believe our story?

Sasha had crouched down by the body and I was vaguely conscious of him peering at it in the daylight now filtering through the trees, and then even touching it. I couldn't be bothered to check him but I heard Stefan snap something, and then Sasha's answer, 'But this one is not yet dead.'

10

I said nothing and he must have thought I didn't believe him. In fact I simply thought he was mistaken. But he insisted, 'She's still alive! Here — give me your hand!'

I shuffled on my bottom across the pine needles, holding out my hand. He grabbed it and guided it to the soft skin of a round throat. When my fingertips touched the flesh I felt a living warmth, and then an almost imperceptible pulse.

Suddenly I remembered a story my brother told me on his last leave, before he was killed in action. A young soldier in his unit had been sentenced to death for cowardice and Tim had to command the firing squad. The victim screamed incessantly as the eight-man squad prepared to kill him and perhaps put them off their aim. After the volley, a doctor examined the body and told Tim, 'He's still alive. Put a bullet in his head.'

Tim said, 'Christ, he's got eight bullets in him.'

'Can't help that. His heart's still beating.'

Apparently none of the bullets had hit a vital spot even though some went right through him. Others hit in such places as a shoulder, an arm, even a foot. Tim told me, 'It just shows how shots can go wild when men are excited or upset. Anyway, I had to use my revolver. I was trembling like a leaf, and I was just going to put a round in the poor devil's ear when he opened one eye and looked at me. I managed to do it, though.'

It was useless for me to try to discover, through the voluminous women's clothes of that period, where this victim had been shot or injured. I tried to think what to do while the Bolsheviks whooped as they threw the first body into the flames, and the terrible stench of burning flesh drifted over to us.

Then I fingered a couple of sovereigns out of my pocket and showed them to Sasha, asking, 'Do you know what these are?'

His eyes widened and he said, 'Gold money?'

'Right. And you know where Dr Stasanowski lives? Then take these to him and tell him if he comes here, to look at this person, I'll give him another ten. Don't tell him she's a Romanov. You can show him the way back here but be very careful. If the Bolsheviks are still around, try to get him to wait till they're gone. Understand?'

He nodded, then asked, 'What will you give me for doing it?'

'Two of these gold sovereigns when you come back.'

He didn't hesitate for an instant. He grabbed the sovereigns from my fingers and disappeared through the trees. Stefan chuckled, 'I hope you see him again,' then nodded towards the motionless girl and asked, 'D'you think she'll live till the doctor comes?'

I told him Timothy's story but he looked doubtful and said, 'A man with all those bullet wounds in him probably wouldn't have lived long anyway.'

I could have kicked him for his pessimism but said nothing. By that time we could see the victim clearly and the morning light showed she had been cruelly bashed about the face and head, perhaps with a riflebutt. Her long thick hair was matted with blood and her blouse, jacket and long heavy skirt were patched with large bloodstains. She was lying awkwardly, just as we'd dropped her, and I tried to straighten her out more comfortably.

The difficulty of finding food in revolutionary Russia had caused Stefan and me to carry whatever we could spare in our backpacks, plus bottles of water. I took my bottle out and trickled a little over the swollen lips, and felt a strange exquisite pleasure when they responded with the tiniest movement.

We could still hear the Bolsheviks and smell their awful bonfire but they became a good deal quieter as the morning wore on. No doubt they were tired and hungover. At about midday we heard the Fiat start and chug away and with a few surreptitious peeps we saw the last of the Bolshies plod off along the road. A long time later I heard they threw some of the burned and half-burned bodies down the mineshaft and threw the rest back into the lorry for disposal elsewhere. Perhaps they lost count and didn't notice, at that time, that one of the bodies was missing.

From time to time I gave the one we'd rescued another sip of water and felt the slight beat of her pulse. Stefan watched cynically but said nothing. The long day dragged on and I'd just about decided that Sasha had run away with the two sovereigns when he came trotting back through the forest with a sack over his shoulder. Stasanowski, on a shaggy pony, was a few yards behind.

Sasha told me, 'Seems everyone in Ekaterinburg has heard about the Reds killing the Romanovs. The Reds say it's only gossip but most people believe it, especially since the Reds are blocking the roads to stop the story getting out.'

I asked, 'How did you get through, then?'

'The patrol we met were all pretty drunk, and they believed me when I told them my sister was having a baby and I was taking the doctor to her.'

Stasanowski dismounted and unstrapped his bag from the pony, and looked down at the victim and said, 'You'd better leave me with her.'

Sasha said, 'I've got some grub in this sack. The doctor bought it with one of those gold pieces.'

The provisions included a bottle of vodka, and I must say I was glad of a good drink of the powerful spirit. After what seemed a very long time Stasanowski came over to us. He looked exhausted and he was grateful for a swig from the vodka bottle. When I asked, 'How's the patient?', he said, 'It's a miracle she's still alive. She's young, and probably strong and healthy before this happened, but I'd have guessed that shock and loss of blood would have finished her.'

'Has she got a chance?'

'Possibly. If she escapes infection.'

He took another swallow of vodka and said, 'I've set a broken right forearm and four broken fingers on her right hand. Of course I haven't any plaster but I've improvised with splints. She has four broken ribs, very painful, but they should heal themselves, and I've replaced a dislocated shoulder.

'She has a broken nose, broken cheek-bones, several teeth knocked out, an ear torn almost in half and bad facial bruising, cuts and so on. I was worried about a possible skull fracture but I think she's escaped that, though her head is badly bruised and swollen and she may have problems with speech, memory and so on.'

I asked, 'How about the shooting?'

'A number of wounds from a standard-issue Nagant pistol. I've taken two bullets from her right thigh. One went through her left shoulder and another through her right bicep, and a couple have passed through the abdomen without hitting the liver or kidneys. Also, a couple skimmed her scalp but cut deep gouges. It's all rather miraculous. I'd say the man appointed as her executioner was either drunk or over-excited, and maybe he'd never handled a pistol before. He simply emptied it into her without really knowing what was happening.'

'How is she now?'

'Deeply unconscious. I gave her a very strong dose of morphine.'

He groped in a pocket and held out a closed fist, saying, 'These were sewn in a seam of her corsets. I think they're diamonds.'

'Could you say who she is?'

'Probably one of the Romanov daughters. She's only about seventeen so I'd guess she's the youngest. Anastasia.'

Sasha handed him a piece of bread and cold bacon and he ate it while I thought about her chances. When I asked bluntly, 'Will she survive?', he answered, 'Possibly. With rest and quiet.'

'Rest and quiet? Where can she find that?'

He looked uncertainly at me and said, 'I want to get my family out of this accursed country and start again elsewhere. If you let me keep these diamonds we could manage it, I think. And I'll help you take Anastasia to my sister's farm, about thirty versts north of here. She raises pigs and goats and so on — when the armies don't steal them.'

I thought for a moment. If Anastasia recovered, Stefan and I might be able to take her to the Allied troops in northern Russia. If she died, we would at least have done what we could for her. Obviously we couldn't just leave her.

The diamonds meant nothing to me and I said, 'All right. How can we take her to your sister?'

'We can manage it on my pony. If necessary I can give her more morphia.'

It's interesting to remember how freely the

doctors prescribed morphia in those days, and how easily available it was in any country that grew poppies. A good many patients became addicts.

I asked, 'When?', and he said, 'Immediately, if you like. We mustn't take chances on the Reds finding her.'

11

Carrying an unconscious body on a pony is not as simple as it sounds but Stefan solved the problem with the dexterity typical of a seaman in the Royal Navy. Stasanowski carried an army blanket rolled behind his saddle and Stefan rolled Anastasia in this, covering her face and tucking her hair out of sight, and lashed it round her body. He adapted the pony's harness in such a way that she could lie along its back. One of us walked at its head and another on each side, steadying the corpse-like bundle if it seemed likely to slide off. Sasha scouted well on ahead, ready to run back and warn us of hazards on the road.

The great pile of embers, from the fire built by the Bolsheviks, still smoked as we walked past, and the ghastly smell still hung around the clearing. I didn't want to know what the Reds had done with the remnants of the bodies and, strangely, I felt a need to hurry Anastasia past the spot to prevent her from knowing what had happened to her family.

A distance of thirty versts meant about twenty miles, which seemed a long way as the pony ambled stolidly along the rough road. The long twilight began again and after a couple of hours I felt I was walking in my sleep. I was grateful when Stasanowski said, 'I'd better check on Anastasia. Why don't we rest awhile?'

We found a spot off the road where we'd be hidden behind trees, and lifted Anastasia carefully down to the ground. I turned away as Stasanowski unwrapped the blanket and began to check on her injuries, but I saw that her clothes looked like a collection of blood-stained rags because he'd had to cut them open and then wrap them round her again, while her face was covered by a loose blanket. Altogether she looked a pretty pathetic bundle, but I'd begun to feel a protective stirring towards her. When Stasanowski finished his work I asked, 'How is she?', and he muttered, 'Not good. We can still hope, though.'

We decided to rest through the brief hours of darkness and I fell almost instantly into an exhausted sleep, but snapped awake at sunrise and found the others already stirring. We secured Anastasia on the pony again and plodded onwards. The rough narrow road, winding ahead of us over the hills and amongst the trees, led us past an occasional hut or cottage and even through a small village, but the few people who saw us pass watched without speaking. There was nothing to tell them whether we were Red or White or anything in between and it obviously seemed wiser to ignore us.

Then, as we travelled along a lonely stretch of road, Sasha came running back to us with the warning, 'Horsemen ahead — four of them.'

There seemed no option but to keep moving along, pausing only when they rode up to us. They wore the usual conglomeration of uniform and civilian clothing, and carried carbines and revolvers. They wore red badges in their caps, and the only way to distinguish their leader was that he rode a little ahead of them.

He was a burly, bearded character, who took his time about extracting and lighting a *papyrossi* while his small suspicious eyes studied us. Finally he blew out smoke, nodded towards the bundle on the pony, and asked, 'Who's that, then?'

To my astonishment, Stasanowski answered gravely, 'My daughter.'

The Red guffawed, 'What's wrong with her, then? Drunk?'

'Dead.'

'Ah. Happening to lots of people these days. So where are you taking her?'

'To the home of my sister, to . . . dispose of her properly.'

The Red nodded carelessly, sucking at his cigarette as he studied the rest of us. Stefan and I looked scruffy, dishevelled and unshaven enough to match any of the countless wanderers of that period, while Sasha looked like any other little boy. Perhaps his presence helped to convince the cavalry-man we were just another family group.

I was expecting the usual demand for 'Papers!' and wondering how we'd talk our way out of it. But he simply took a last drag at his cigarette, flicked it away, clicked to his horse and told us, 'On your way, then, comrades.'

Their hoofbeats had died away along the road behind us before I could relax and say to Stasanowski, 'I admire your presence of mind. I wouldn't have known what to say to them.'

He shrugged, saying modestly, 'Just came to me. And after all, she may indeed be dead by this time.'

The nature of the forest had been changing, from the darkness of pine to the green of birch, beech and ash trees. Eventually Stasanowski led us off the road on to a track, no wider than that worn down by a pair of cartwheels, which ran a few hundred yards to the farm which his sister, Maria Nikitoy, had inherited from her husband. The farmhouse was a solid 'log cabin' type of building set amidst various sheds, stalls, sties and vegetable gardens.

Maria was a hard-faced woman of middle age, tall and strong and with hands like a labourer's. Her sons had been conscripted, her daughters had married and left home, and she ran the farm with the help of two ancient peasants, Vladimir and Tomasz.

She received us with astonishment and reluctance. Stasanowski took her aside, talking to her fast and urgently, and at first she seemed unresponsive. But at last she began to nod and he returned to us and said, 'I told Maria you would pay her well, in real money, not Bolshevik paper, for looking after our patient. Agreed?'

I said, 'Yes, of course.'

'Then we must get the poor girl inside immediately.'

When we carried Anastasia inside she felt so stiff and unresponsive I wondered whether she was still alive. Maria showed us into a little room at the back of the house, and Stasanowski told me, 'Leave her with Maria and me. We can undress and wash her now, and I can attend to her injuries more carefully.'

After what seemed like a long time Maria reappeared, carrying Anastasia's clothing.

The garments were stained and stiff with blood and cut about from the assault on her and from Stasanowski cutting them off her. Maria said, 'I'm going to burn these so that nobody will ask any questions. I've some old clothes of my daughter's I can remake for the girl. And you'd better take care of this.'

She handed me a little leather bag. I could feel the weight and texture of the contents, then looked inside and saw the glint of jewels of various sizes. Maria said, 'They were sewn into her clothing, apart from those you already gave to my brother.'

I nodded, impressed by their honesty, and asked, 'How is she?'

Her eyes filled, and tears looked somehow incongruous on her weathered face. 'Poor child. Those who did that to her are worse than animals. But my brother hopes she will survive. He's told me what to do and left what medicines he can spare.'

When Stasanowski emerged he told us, 'I think we can be more optimistic, but she must not be moved for a while.'

He insisted on leaving us, saying, 'I have more patients, and the Reds will become suspicious if I'm away too long. I'll be telling them I've been on a visit to my sister, for family reasons.'

When he trotted away on his pony we

began a strange period in which we knew little of the world outside though we could guess what was happening. Sometimes the summer air reverberated with artillery fire like distant thunder, and Maria kept a watchful eye on the main road. She told us, 'Last year we were looted by both sides. That's why we now keep our animals deep in the forest.'

We helped her as much as we could and survived on the same diet as she and her helpers: potatoes and other vegetables from her garden, goat's milk, a little meat from her smokehouse. Such items as tea, coffee, bread and sugar were forgotten luxuries.

Maria proved a good nurse for Anastasia. She tended her in such ways as her brother had advised and fed her on such things as potatoes mashed in goat's milk. On the third day she told me, 'The poor child is fully conscious today but she doesn't say anything. I don't know whether that's because she won't or can't. I think she doesn't know what's happened to her or where she is.'

I soon trusted Maria enough to discuss my next moves with her. Tomasz and Vladimir had contacts among the timberfellers and other denizens of the forest and they passed on a mixture of fact and rumour. They told us that Ekaterinburg would soon fall to the

Whites and that the hills were infested with renegades and deserters. The Bolsheviks had announced the 'execution' of Nicholas but said nothing about their murder of his family and servants.

I told Maria I hoped to reach Murmansk or Archangel, where Allied troops had landed, and she pointed them out on a school atlas. They both looked dauntingly far away, at least a thousand miles. But I'd made up my mind not to surrender Anastasia to the Reds or hand her over as a political puppet to the Whites. I'd been ordered to rescue the Romanovs and it was my duty to save the last member of the family.

Maria never asked me why Stefan and I were in Russia, or how I'd become involved with Anastasia. I think she simply accepted the situation as part of the madness then gripping the world, and her own country in particular.

Soon after that she heard a rumour which made her set us all to work, digging up potatoes and turnips and other root vegetables and carrying them, with other surplus food, away to a cache in the forest. She had three elderly horses and a mule on the farm and Vladimir took them all away except for one old mare. He told me, 'We had a good cart once but the Reds stole it!'

The rumour proved correct when a White Army foraging party, led by a Lieutenant Strogov, came along the road. Their two wagons were already well laden with produce commandeered from other farms but they took everything they could find, and even led the old mare away. Maria protested, 'She's too old to ride!', to which Strogov answered, 'Then we'll eat her.'

He and his men didn't look very different from the Bolshevik patrol we'd encountered, though he did wear an officer's cap and his khaki uniform blouse had shoulder-boards with rank badges. The Bolsheviks, at that time, forbade such marks of social discrimination. He was a lean, hard-bitten man with sardonic eyes and a nasty twist to his mouth, and he smiled cynically as he flicked through our papers. The Whites disliked the British at that time, because of our change of mind about providing sanctuary for the Romanovs.

He asked, 'What are you doing here?', and I told him we'd left Ekaterinburg before the Whites attacked the town, and found refuge on the farm while we decided what to do next.

'You couldn't stay and help us capture Ekaterinburg?'

'That's not our metier.'

He grunted 'Huh!' just as we heard a yowl

of pain, and a couple of Whites dragged in Vladimir with a split lip and bleeding nose. One of them said, 'This old peasant won't tell us, your honour, but I'll bet he knows where more grub is hidden.'

Strogov sneered, 'Oh, let him go. We mustn't let the British see us ill-treating peasants.'

Vladimir tottered off, while Strogov pulled a folded sheet of paper from his breast pocket. It carried a smudged photograph of Iurovsky and the words WANTED FOR TREASON AND MURDER. The text offered an absurdly enormous reward in roubles.

Strogov asked, 'Have you come across this man?' and I shook my head. When he first appeared I'd felt inclined to tell him about Anastasia. I'd felt that was really the right thing to do. But I was rapidly developing an intense dislike for him, confirmed when he fingered the notice and said, 'If I ever catch this bastard I'll torture him to death with my own hands.'

He was starting to say something else when the sound of dissent came from the back of the house, with Maria's voice rising over all. Seconds later she came storming in, followed by a couple of Whites. One exclaimed, 'Your honour, there's a girl in bed back there,' and Maria cried, 'She's been in an accident and she's very ill! You leave her alone!'

Strogov scoffed, 'Raped and beaten up by the Reds, I suppose. Plenty of girls have that kind of accident,' just as a sergeant appeared in the doorway, saluted, and reported, 'We've loaded up everything we can find, your honour.'

Maria said bitterly, 'You're worse than the Reds,' to which Strogov answered, 'That's why we'll beat them.'

I followed him out into the farmyard where an orderly held his horse. As usual I found that duty was overcoming personal inclination, and I'd reluctantly decided I should tell him about Anastasia. But as he mounted he looked down on me and said, 'There's something funny about this place but I've no time to look into it now. You'd better be on your way before I do.'

I almost uttered the Russian equivalent of 'Get stuffed!' but kept my mouth shut. I watched them leaving and returned to the house, where Maria asked me, 'You didn't tell him?'

I shook my head. She said, 'Good,' then, 'She's not ready to move yet. She doesn't even know what's happening,' and then, very firmly, 'The Whites won't win this war. Too many of them are like Strogov: contemptuous of ordinary people. God knows what they'd make of Ana if she got into their hands.'

The next two or three weeks dragged past with increasing anxiety. Stefan and I spent much of our time in the woods, guarding the cache of food. Despite Strogov's threat neither he nor any other Whites reappeared, and we heard rumours that the Reds had rallied for a new offensive, but I was desperate to be moving again.

Maria delayed approval for Ana to travel and on the one occasion I saw her I understood why. She lay motionless in bed, face covered by a loose bandage except for closed eyes, and when Maria said softly, 'Ana, someone to see you,' stared at me with blue eyes that showed a strange mixture of fear and incomprehension. After a few moments she shut her eyes again. But Maria helped me to plan our travel, saying, 'You should head north-west out of the Urals to the Kumar River, and go along it to the city of Perm. You may be able to take a train there to carry you part of the way to the coast.'

Day by day she reported small steps in Ana's progress. She had stood up for a minute or two, spoken a few words, managed to wash herself, and so on. When Maria took me in to her again she looked at me warily but not fearfully. I asked Maria, 'Have you told her who I am?'

'Just that you're an Englishman who wants to help her.'

'Does she understand that?'

'I'm not sure she even knows who she is or what's happened to her.'

The day came when Ana took a few steps outside. Maria had washed and dressed her long, thick, dark-blonde hair and dressed her in the clothes she had adapted for her. She looked normal except for the veil she insisted on wearing round her face and the eyes looking over it, which showed only a kind of wariness.

Maria agreed Ana was almost fit to travel, and I said, 'There is a problem, though. She has no papers if anyone stops us.'

Maria said, 'Yes, I've thought about that and there's a simple answer. You should marry her.'

I thought she was making rather a poor joke and managed a smile, but she said, 'I'm serious. My brother — my other brother — is a priest in the cathedral at Perm. I'll come with you and explain the situation.'

'But would he — well, issue a marriage certificate?'

'I think he'd do anything to help a daughter of the Emperor. He hates the Reds and he's a very old-fashioned man.'

She was moving faster than I liked and I

asked, 'But what would she use for identification on the way to Perm, if the Reds stop us?'

'She can carry the birth certificate of my daughter Rossiya.'

I was a little ashamed of myself for bringing up so many objections. A Royal Navy man was supposed to solve problems without brooding over the difficulties. But I said, 'Aren't your daughters older than she is? Wouldn't the birth date seem wrong?'

'I never told you about Rossiya. She died last year of pneumonia, aged seventeen. That would be just right, eh?'

Thoughts whirled through my head, such as: What would people think if I returned to England married to the girl I was supposed to rescue? Did I want to be married to a girl with no family and a mass of problems, plus a battered face and body? If I did marry her, and managed to get her to England, would I be allowed to divorce a girl related to the British royal family?

Plus: Why would Ana need a marriage certificate if Maria could provide her with a birth certificate?

I asked Maria that question and she answered, 'Because a marriage certificate would give her a reason for accompanying you.'

Thinking I was playing a trump card I asked, 'But what would *your* reason be for travelling with us to Perm?'

She gave me her rare smile. 'That I am to be your mother-in-law, of course. And that I wish to witness her marriage, by my brother, in the Russian Orthodox Church.'

I heard myself utter another 'But' when I asked, 'But how can you leave your farm?'

'I've told you — I think the Reds will win. Not just for the reason I gave you but because they have a single strong leadership. The Whites have too many leaders, often jealous of each other and sometimes fighting for personal gain.'

'So how does that affect your farm?'

'The Reds aim to finish private ownership and establish collective farms. So I will lose my farm anyway.'

I opened my mouth to ask more questions but shut it again. I thought she would have logical answers for all of them.

And in due course Vladimir brought the elderly mule, which had the unlikely name of Ballerina, back out of the woods. Maria produced an ancient side-saddle and harness, Sasha was set to work on cleaning them, and Maria helped Ana limp out for a trial ride. She needed help in mounting but, once in the saddle, sat there confidently. I suppose she was taught by a royal riding-master.

After that everything moved along fairly easily until the morning when, at early sunrise, we left the farm. Vladimir and Tomasz, left in charge, watched our little procession wend its way into the forest. Maria, who was familiar with the woodland tracks for about a day's journey into the forest, was the leader. Sasha led Ballerina, who was laden with a bag of potatoes together with Ana, who wore the clothes Maria had altered for her. A wide-brimmed hat and veil, together with her long thick hair, obscured her head and face. Stefan and I, carrying extra bags of provisions as well as our backpacks, tramped after her. She rode fairly easily to start with but riding soon tired and hurt her, and she alternated spells on muleback with limping along with the rest of us. On one such occasion I found myself walking beside her. I realized, strangely, I had not so far spoken to her without Maria as intermediary. I had to make a slight effort to ask, 'Are you getting on all right?' and I might as well have saved my breath. She did not answer or even look at me. But a little later on, when we came to a tangle of branches across the track, I held out my hand to help her and she took it hesitantly, but drew hers away as soon as we were in the clear again.

The forest was so quiet and peaceful, apart from the morning and evening chorus of the birds, that we almost forgot the conflict not far away. We had occasional reminders in the form of small parties glimpsed through the trees, either deserters or refugees, but they all steered clear of us.

We were heading for a river port where, in more peaceful times, paddle steamers loaded passengers and cargo for transport down to Perm. We hoped we could still find such transport when, after several weary days of tramping and camping through the forest, we came to a well-travelled road leading to the port. As we progressed along this we found ourselves part of an increasing stream of refugees, halted time after time at roadblocks manned by officious Bolsheviks. We didn't know whether they were Cheka, Red Army or some other authority. Many Bolsheviks seemed to pride themselves on a bearded, dishevelled appearance hung about with weaponry.

But they seemed to be impressed by the British passports, with their lion and unicorn seals, which Stefan and I showed them, and they waved Sasha and Maria and Ana through as our companions. All went well until we came to the final block, at the entrance to the port area, where half a dozen

Reds lounged around and one pointed to Ballerina with the command, 'Transport animals must be surrendered for military use! By order, Bilimbaevsk Soviet!'

I was sorry to see Ballerina led away, while Stefan and I divided the remnants of the sack of potatoes to carry between us, but I'd known we couldn't take her on the river boat. The guard who had commandeered her glanced at our passports and then demanded, 'Who are these women?'

Maria spoke up with, 'I am Maria Nicolaevna Nikitoy and this is my daughter Rossiya. We are travelling to Perm.'

'What are you doing with these Englishmen?'

'Helping and guiding them, cooking and so on.'

He laughed coarsely. 'Yes, I can guess what you mean by 'so on'. Let's see your papers.'

He examined them, demanding, 'What's your business in Perm?'

'My brother Anatoly is a priest in the cathedral there.'

He grimaced as though she'd said something disgusting. 'You know the God-houses are being closed and their lackeys dismissed?'

'Of course. But he's my brother and we haven't seen each other for a long time.'

He turned his attention to Ana, sneering,

'Why are you hiding your pretty face, then?'

She said nothing and he moved closer to her, then snatched suddenly at the veil covering her face. Stefan exclaimed, 'Jesus!' when he saw the shattered features and piteous eyes, before she jerked the veil up again. The Bolshevik spat, 'Pah! Who did that to her?'

Maria snapped, 'Men, of course! Men without feelings or pity!'

He ignored that and glanced at Sasha. I thought he might demand papers for the boy but so many children had been orphaned, lost or abandoned that neither side seemed to spare a thought for them until they were old enough to be raped or conscripted.

The Bolshevik waved a dirty hand at us, saying, 'Go on, then, filthy bourgeois, filthy foreigners.'

We walked through on to the wharf, where a large paddle steamer lay alongside with smoke drifting from her funnel. Two large barges were tied up astern of her, ready to tow downstream.

The steamer and barges were already laden with passengers, while long queues still hoped to be allowed aboard. I saw our chances were pretty slight and I queue-jumped relentlessly, ignoring the shouts and insults from those preceding us and ensuring our party kept close together. When I reached the trio of crewmen guarding the gangway one of them shouted, 'We're full, comrade! Overloaded! Just casting off!'

I pressed a golden sovereign in his hand and said, 'Tell your captain he can have ten of these if he lets five more aboard.' His eyes widened when he saw the coin but he demanded, 'Then give me one for each of my mates, too!'

I was taking a risk because, for all I knew, the captain was a devout Bolshevik who scorned bribery, or there might be a Commissar in charge of the riverboat. But after an agonizing wait the crewman returned and said, 'Captain says all right. Give me the money and you can come aboard.'

The fury and despair of those left behind exploded in volleys of stones, threats and insults as the crew cast off the moorings and the big paddle wheels began to turn. The river boat had been berthed with bows heading upstream, perhaps because there'd been some intention of visiting a port further up, and this gave her skipper a difficult manoeuvre. The river, running down from the Urals, has a strong current even in midsummer, and he had to turn the boat across that with the two heavy barges in tow.

The boat had just turned away from the

wharf when a car came speeding through the gates, honking at the guards to get out of the way. But the thick queue had broken up into a chaotic crowd, stopping the car just inside the gates, and three men jumped out and began to force their way through.

Their leader, in a plain khaki uniform, reached the edge of the wharf while the river boat was making its turn. The paddles were threshing noisily, one going ahead and the other going astern and they drowned out whatever the newcomer was trying to shout to the crew. But I heard a bellow from the bridge of, 'No more! Full up! Can't turn back!'

Then Sasha, standing next to me amongst the press of passengers at the rail, said, 'That's Iakov Iurovsky. Wonder where he got the uniform? Angry, isn't he?'

I saw that the man gesturing and shouting angrily was indeed the one I'd last seen in the Fiat lorry in the clearing in the forest. He was so angry that he drew his revolver and fired several shots at the riverboat, but she was moving out of range and her skipper responded with a derisive toot on the whistle.

But I didn't like the feel of Iurovsky's sudden appearance and I said, 'What the hell's he doing here?'

Stefan said, 'Probably just wants a free trip

to Perm. He wouldn't want to drive there, not with these country roads the way they are.'

Maria said, 'It's probably just coincidence.'

I told her, 'I wouldn't like to think he knows we're aboard, though. He could telegraph to Perm — or even telephone.'

She laughed at that. 'You'd be lucky to find a telegraph pole still standing. Either the Whites or the Reds have chopped most of them down.'

As the river boat threshed her way downriver I felt, for the first time, gratitude for Russia's immense distances. If Iurovsky was indeed pursuing us — and there was really no reason to think he was — we had a good start on him.

Passengers on the river boat were a strange mixture. A good many were Red Army sick and wounded, plus a rough-and-ready medical staff which seemed to spend as much time boozing and yarning as they did looking after their patients. There was an entire agitprop contingent, ready to spout propaganda at any moment, plus a number of Bolshevik officials and other civilians. And a great many were refugees, both Red and White and ranging from individuals to entire families, who had fled the combat areas in the hope of a better life elsewhere.

There was little to eat on board but the

riverboat stopped several times on the trip down the river to take on wood fuel stacked at villages along the banks. The peasants there sold the passengers such items as eggs, potatoes and fruit, and it seemed to me they showed dislike for both Reds and Whites. Maria said drily, 'They think the revolution is city business and nothing to do with country-folk who know how to look after themselves.'

I was still not reconciled to her plans for my marriage to Ana and I asked her, 'Is it really necessary? Couldn't you just come along with us and look after her? I've got enough money for all of us and I could pay you well for it.'

She told me bluntly, 'We've been lucky so far. We still haven't run into the kind of communist official who likes to make big trouble. My brother told me about some of them. He might let you and Stefan go but what would become of Ana?'

She paused, then said, 'And I must try to help my brother Anatoly, in Perm. The Reds are starting to persecute the clergy and if he's thrown out on the world he wouldn't know how to look after himself.'

She smiled then, and nodded towards Sasha, who was leaning on the rail chatting to Stefan, and said, 'And I can't desert him. He's already calling me 'Mama'.'

12

I expected cross-examination from the Bolsheviks when we arrived at Perm but they were too busy getting their own people ashore to worry about the rest of us. We tramped through the streets to the Cathedral of St Michael and St Mark, where Maria found her brother was conducting services for St Bartholomew's Day and wouldn't be able to see us for an hour or so. I was eager to arrange our next move, the rail journey northwards, and so Stefan and I walked off to the railway station.

That was the time the Bolshevik theorists decided to abolish money, substituting ration cards for such necessities as food and clothing. Accommodation, transport and other services were to be free of charge. The result was chaotic, as we discovered when we arrived at the station. An even bigger mob than usual, largely composed of people who decided to take a trip at government expense, besieged the ticket office.

But we found that private enterprise still flourished. A sharp-eyed individual spotted us as different from other would-be travellers and he approached us with some polite remarks about our destination. When I said, 'We want to go as far north as possible,' he said, 'Ah!', and invited us to have drinks in the station buffet where — despite the no-money project — we had to pay cash for watered vodka in dirty glasses.

Our new acquaintance introduced himself as Valenti and said, 'The furthest north you can travel by rail is to the railhead at Kotlas, on the River North Dvina. That's about halfway to Archangel and you may be able to board a riverboat for the rest of the way.' He asked, 'You must be foreigners, eh? Heading for the Allied troops landing at Archangel?' and when I said nothing he shrugged and said, 'Ah well — none of my business. How many of you will be travelling?'

'Three.'

'And how will you pay for it?'

I'd prepared for this question by fumbling a sovereign into my hand. His eyes sparkled when I displayed the gold coin but he said only, 'Excellent. All right, I'll see what I can do. Meet me here same time day after tomorrow.'

I noticed Stefan's surly stare after him as he walked away, and asked, 'What's the matter?'

He took his time about extracting and

lighting a *papyrossi*, grimaced at the cloud of smoke he exhaled, grumbled, 'I'd give anything for a proper fag,' and asked, 'Man to man, then?'

'Of course.'

'Well, I dunno why we're taking all this trouble over Ana. We were supposed to help the Romanovs escape but that's gone down the drain. What's the point of taking a lot of chances to get her to England? I reckon the Whites can't be far away and we could just hand her over, and buzz off home the same way we came.' He gulped another lungful of smoke and blew it out again. 'Even if you get the poor kid to England they won't thank you. She's gone dotty if you ask me, and no wonder.

'But she's the heiress to the throne of Russia. The bloody country's fallen apart and it will take a miracle to put it back together again. And I reckon you'll be putting your head in a noose with this idea of marrying her.'

He finished his cigarette and said, 'Why don't you just give Maria half of the money we've got and ask her to look after Ana. I'll bet she'd do whatever's best for her.'

By that time I'd been almost ten years in the Royal Navy and I'd given and received countless orders, obeying them instinctively and expecting obedience. Questioning an order was unthinkable. Stefan's remarks did not exactly add up to that but I felt as though they did. I said, 'My orders are to help the Romanovs escape. Ana's the only one left but the orders still hold good.'

Our eyes met and I saw something in his that had never been there before. Ever since childhood I had been the leader and he the follower, but I sensed he was starting to wonder about that. But he answered, 'Aye, aye, sir,' in proper Royal Navy style.

We made our way back to the cathedral, where a verger showed us into a bare little office. Maria was there with her brother Anatoly, whose mild eyes watched us gravely from a face almost obscured by hair and beard. The man next to him was even hairier, with shoulder-length hair and a beard smothering his features.

I sensed something was wrong even before Maria said, 'This is Brother Maxim from the monastery at Ekaterinburg. The Reds burned it down, and drove all the monks out on to the roads, shortly before the Whites fought their way into the city.'

Anatoly added, 'Maxim and some others made their way here a couple of days ago. I'm sorry to say he has bad news for you.' Maxim said dolefully, 'The Cheka arrested Dr

Eugene Stasanowski, when someone reported him for trying to sell a diamond. Now they accuse him of helping one of the Romanovs to escape.'

I asked, 'How do they know that?'

'Everyone in Ekaterinburg knows the Cheka murdered the Romanovs and their servants, even though they only admit to executing Emperor Nicholas. I've also heard the Reds tried to burn up the bodies in the forest, and threw the remnants down a mineshaft. Then, when it became clear that the Whites would recapture Ekaterinburg, the Cheka decided to extract the bodies from the mineshaft and take them elsewhere, so that the Whites wouldn't know what happened to them. But when they did so they found the remains of only ten bodies, when there should have been eleven.'

Maria said, 'But I believe my brother left Ekaterinburg before the Whites returned. It was hard to keep in touch but the last time I saw him — when these people brought Ana to us — he told me he had enough money to get out of Russia and meant to leave immediately. I didn't ask him how or why — it's best not to know these things.'

Maxim told her, 'He wasn't arrested in Ekaterinburg. He and his family were on their way to Omsk. He tried to sell the diamond on the way there, in a town still occupied by the Reds. I'm told that an officer of the Cheka, a man named Iurovsky, heard about it when someone reported your brother.'

I asked, 'Are you saying that the Cheka . . . well, somehow got the truth out of Dr Stasanowski?'

'So I was told. The person who told me his story said Iurovsky suspected the doctor of removing the diamond from the body of one of the Romanovs. Iurovsky took Dr Stasanowski's two children away from him and their mother and threatened to kill them if he did not tell the truth.'

I dared not look at Maria. She clasped her head in her hands, looking down at the table, and after a minute asked, 'What happened to them?'

Maxim said in his doleful voice, 'I'm sorry to say I cannot tell you.'

She said almost calmly, 'I think Eugene would have told Iurovsky everything in the hope of saving his family. But the Cheka has no mercy and I doubt whether I'll ever see them again.'

We were all silent until Anatoly began to murmur a prayer, and Maxim joined in. Maria said nothing until they finished, when she raised her head and looked at me. Her face was as stern as ever when she said,

'Anatoly is prepared to perform the wedding ceremony according to the rites of our church, and he can issue a marriage certificate, but he won't agree to Ana using a false name and pretending to be my daughter.'

'You know her real name?'

'Yes, of course. Eugene told me, and I've told Anatoly.'

'Then — '

I was about to voice what seemed the obvious objection but she guessed what I'd say, and interrupted with 'The name of Romanov is very common in Russia. It simply means 'son of Roma', which is a favourite Christian name. Roman Koshkin adopted the name, for the imperial dynasty, when he was elected Tsar of Russia three centuries ago.'

But I asked Anatoly, 'Will you get into trouble if you marry me to Ana Romanov?'

He answered, 'The Bolsheviks are the ones who will get into trouble. They hate God and he will punish them.'

'But will the Reds punish you for this.'

He shrugged. 'What do I care for their punishment? My conscience is clear and my soul belongs to God.'

As a kind of final effort I said, 'I'd be happier about this if I thought Ana understood what's happening,' but Maria replied, 'The important thing is to give her a chance to get out of this unfortunate country, so that she may recover somewhere peaceful.'

She and Anatoly looked calmly at me, awaiting my decision, and with a feeling like that I'd experienced when jumping off a sinking ship, I said, 'All right, then.'

Maria told me, 'Anatoly has arranged for us to stay here for as long as we need. There is plenty of room because a number of the cathedral staff have returned to their homes.'

We were accommodated in a kind of priory behind the cathedral. We lived in something like monks' cells, and ate in the company of men and women who, like ourselves, were being provided with refuge. The food was simple but sufficient and the atmosphere calm and quiet, very different from the feelings which prompted vandals to paint such graffiti as 'God is on the losing side' on the outside walls of the cathedral. But I noticed the building still attracted a steady stream of worshippers and many carried gifts for the clergy, if only a couple of potatoes.

Maria asked me for money to pay for the wedding and also told me, 'Anatoly knows an . . . official who will provide a civil marriage certificate. Together with the cathedral certificate it should answer any questions, but the official will need a tip shall we say.'

As I gave her what she needed I said, 'I wouldn't have thought Anatoly knew anyone like that.'

'Oh, they've been friends for years. Some members of the old official service have sworn allegiance to new masters, simply to stay in employment.'

My next obligation was the follow-up with the man we'd met on the railway station. Stefan and I went there at the appointed time, half-expecting not to see him, and I was shocked to see him accompanied by a man in Red Army uniform. I almost turned away, but he smiled and beckoned us to follow into the refreshment room. His companion, in the style of the Red Army at that time, wore no rank badges. Bolshevik theory was that nobody had the right to display superiority over anyone else. But the soldier wore a holstered revolver, which displayed his authority as effectively as any badges of rank, plus a challenging scowl as though he was prepared to dislike us. He had a broad flat face with skin so coarse it seemed possible to count the pores in it, including those which sprouted ill-shaven whiskers. Valenti introduced him with, 'This is Kyril, who will command the next train to Kotlas.'

Kyril sneered, 'I hear you're some kind of foreigners, trying to run away from communist Russia.'

I said, 'We're simply trying to return to our own country.'

'Valenti said there'd be three of you. Where's the other one?'

'She'll be my wife. Didn't seem necessary to bring her today.'

Valenti interrupted smoothly, 'Kyril might be able to find space for you on the train. It all depends.'

'Depends on what?'

'Well, it's customary for civilian passengers on military trains, unless they have official authority, to contribute to the finances of the Red Army.'

I almost smirked at that way of putting it but answered politely, 'Yes, of course. How much would be suitable?'

That began a round of bargaining, accompanied by watered vodka at our expense, which ended with their acceptance of forty sovereigns. When I handed over the little cylindrical packages Kyril's tongue slid over his thick lips as though he was tasting the deal and finding it satisfactory. He said, 'I'll see you at six in the morning, day after tomorrow,' and, 'How will you get from Kotlas to Archangel?'

'I'm hoping to find a riverboat down the North Dvina River.'

He scoffed, 'You'll be lucky!'

I'd had about enough of Kyril but managed to restrain a sharp reply. He lumbered to his feet and rolled way with Valenti, who gave us a polite farewell smile. Stefan said, 'Fancy an army officer taking a bribe in public!' and I said, 'I only hope he keeps his side of the bargain!'

On my wedding day Maria gave me a signed and stamped certificate headed 'Perm Soviet' and attesting Benjamin Arthur Knyve had been married that day to Anastasia Romanov. While I was looking at it I remembered I had promised to pay her for all her efforts, and gave her fifty sovereigns. When I asked awkwardly, 'Is that enough?', her eyes filled and she gulped, 'It's a life-saver.'

The wedding ceremony took place in a side-chapel of the cathedral. Stefan and I had managed to buy some secondhand clothing which was rather more respectable than the garb which was stained and rumpled by our exertions since leaving England. I felt very self-conscious when Anatoly entered in ceremonial vestments plus another priest and a pallid young server. When Maria and Ana appeared I saw that Maria had obtained a fairly new street dress for the bride, together with a veil covering her face and flowing down to her shoulders, and surmounted with a chaplet of flowers.

I'd given little thought to Ana's feelings about the wedding. I'd become accustomed to regarding her as a kind of non-person who had to be organized for her own good. Years later, when I asked her how Maria had persuaded her to marry me, she answered, 'I don't really remember. You know the condition I was in and I simply did whatever I was told. I think Maria told me that the best thing for me was to marry you and so I simply did it.'

For my part I'd never given much thought to marriages. In those days the Royal Navy frowned upon marriage for young officers, believing that a wife prevented a young man from devoting himself wholeheartedly to his duty. The war had modified such beliefs but many senior officers still deplored marriage for their juniors. When I took my place beside Ana I wondered what my father and his contemporaries would think about this wedding and told myself that, after all, it was my duty.

The Russian ceremony, including the exchange of rings provided by Maria, seemed to me to be longer and more complex than that of the Church of England but at last it came to an end. I signed the marriage register, Maria guided Ana in doing so, and Anatoly signed the certificate and gave it to me. Maria took Ana and me by the hands and said, 'I've arranged a little celebration for you. Come along.'

She led us to a little room where a plate of plain cakes stood on a table with a bottle of wine and some glasses. Maria poured out the wine and handed the glasses round, and proposed a toast to Ana and me. I felt it was appropriate for me to slip an arm around Ana's shoulders but she flinched away from me.

When we'd drunk some wine and munched the tasteless little cakes, Maria set her empty glass on the table and said, 'We are going now and I'm taking Sasha with me, and he understands I shall be looking after him. I've arranged for you three to keep your rooms here until you leave in the morning. We wish you good fortune and bid you farewell.'

She led Sasha out of the room before I could say anything, and the priests bowed to us and followed her. Stefan and I were left open-mouthed with astonishment. He hurried to the door as though to follow them and demand an explanation but I said, 'Never mind. Let them go. Maria's worked out what she wants to do and we must go our own way. The first thing is to make darn sure we catch that train in the morning.'

13

I was so anxious not to miss the train that I knocked the others up too early, and wondered whether Ana could dress herself and pack her few possessions. But she managed to do so and limped gamely along between Stefan and me on the walk to the railway station. She said nothing and I had nothing to say to her.

We found the appropriate platform in the railway station was already crowded with Red Army men, a regiment at least, looking smarter and better equipped than most of their comrades I'd seen so far. They'd just been issued with a breakfast of black bread, which they were sharing with friends and relations who'd come to see them off. Their weapons and equipment cluttered the platform and like any other crowd of young men in similar circumstances they were noisily cheerful.

I spotted Kyril chatting to some older men, but although he met my eye he ignored me. We didn't know where to position ourselves to board the train but saw a group of civilians huddled together at one end of the platform and pushed through to join them. They included a middle-aged man whose clothes looked as though he'd been rolled through a rubbish dump. He was hatless, and his face was swollen and discoloured with old and new bruises including a black eye. He watched interestedly as we approached and nodded when I asked, 'Are you going to Kotlas?'

He looked curiously at Ana, whose broad-brimmed hat and veil concealed her face, and when Stefan and I exchanged a few words in English he asked, in a strong American accent, 'Are you guys Britishers?'

Stefan answered, 'Yes — are you a Yank?'

He laughed at that, just as a train came clanking along the track alongside the platform. I didn't know where we were supposed to board it but when the English-speaking man pushed his way into a carriage I presumed we could follow. The train wasn't big enough to hold everyone waiting for it and a throng of soldiers was trying to push into the carriage we'd entered when Stefan exclaimed, 'Christ, there's Iurovsky!'

I'd just found space for Ana and me on the side of the carriage furthest from the platform. Stefan was standing, with his back to me, and I couldn't see past him and other passengers to the platform. But I heard, through an open window, the voice I remembered as Iurovsky's shouting, 'Everyone out! Empty the train!'

That was followed by a babble of voices protesting, laughing and ironically cheering. Iurovsky bawled above the din, 'Out! Out! Everyone out on the platform!' but then I heard Kyril bellow, 'Shut your mouth! Impossible! Go away!'

This was emphasized by a screech from the engine whistle. The soldiers in our carriage became a gaping audience crammed along the windows, blocking my view of the platform, but I heard Kyril shout 'We already waited a week for this train!' and Iurovsky say something about his authority as an official of the Cheka. Kyril answered, 'Show me your order to empty the train!'

'I'd no time to obtain one! I only arrived here an hour ago!'

'Then stand back!'

'This is a military train but there are civilians aboard!'

'No reason why not — we can fit them in!'

'I insist on examining them!'

I hadn't liked Kyril's manner but now I was silently applauding his belligerence as he yelled, 'Lick my arse, Cheka swine! We're leaving!'

'I'll report you to Moscow!'

'And I'll report you for holding up the Red Army on our way to fight the invaders!'

Iurovsky continued yelling while Kyril signalled the train to leave and climbed aboard. Stefan turned to me, chuckling, 'You should have seen Iurovsky — all by himself and looking as though he'd been dragged through a hedge backwards. He must've had a hell of a time getting here.'

But I was impressed by the Cheka man's seeming determination to recapture Ana. He seemed to be acting independently, which might have meant he feared condemnation for letting her escape and was now hunting her single-handedly And it could also mean he'd wrung information out of Vladimir and Tomasz. Or, perhaps, the Red leadership didn't want their murder of the Romanovs to become nationally known, and wanted Iurovsky to catch her without too much publicity.

Whatever the reason, I could do nothing about it. I tried, like all the others, to settle down for the long journey ahead. Ana, despite the jolting and swaying of the train, sat upright in the manner of a well-bred young lady of that era. Some of the young soldiers stared curiously at the hat, veil and long hair concealing her face, but veils were only just going out of fashion and were still not uncommon. There was even a popular superstition that it was unlucky to kiss one's wife through her veil.

The man with the bruised face soon opened conversation with us. He introduced himself as Grigor Peskov, and told us he was the son of a Kotlas merchant in a small way of business. At twenty-one he decided to see the world and emigrated to the USA, where there was plenty of work for strong young men and he rose from builder's labourer to foreman to minor contractor, seeing a good deal of North America as he did so. He learned to speak and write good English and developed an interest in writing for publication, and eventually had articles published in various magazines.

When his father died he returned to Kotlas and took over the business, then expanding because the railway had reached the town. Wartime meant that all war material landed at Archangel and brought up the river had to be sent south through Kotlas, and Grigor benefited accordingly. But the revolution destroyed the business and the Reds called Grigor a capitalist traitor, and eventually brought him to Perm. 'They said the Cheka would screw the truth out of me and I thought I was done for. I've been locked up for most of a year, getting knocked around pretty often, but they've finally decided I'm innocent and let me go.'

I sensed that Ana was also listening to Grigor's story and I wondered whether, like most scions of European royalty, she had been taught English. But I couldn't tell whether she understood Grigor or was simply listening to the sound of his voice.

He was curious about Ana but I fobbed off his questions, telling him only that she was my wife. The journey dragged on with the Siberian landscape rolling past the windows: forests of pine and birch, stretches of open plain, flat farmlands around little villages, rivers idling through swampland. Now and again the train stopped at small towns, where some of the civilian passengers dodged out, and I wondered what they'd paid Kyril for their journey. We'd brought some food with us, mostly cold boiled potatoes, and Grigor was effusively grateful when we gave him a share. Ana nibbled hers under her veil, chewing cautiously with her damaged teeth.

We were stiff, grimy, bored and sleepless after a thirty hour journey when the train reached Kotlas. The soldiers formed up and marched off to the riverboats awaiting them and Kyril gave us a farewell glance. I expected Bolshevik officials to challenge us but nobody took any notice of us. Grigor lingered uncertainly, then asked, 'How will you get to Archangel?'

'I'm hoping to buy passages in a river boat.'

'Not a chance. The Red Army's commandeered all of them.'

'Then we'll buy or hire horses.'

'If you can find any. The Red Army's taken them too.'

His attitude annoyed me. 'Then we'll walk, dammit!'

'Yes, you might get there before the winter freeze sets in.' He rasped a hand over his stubbled face, then said, 'I want to get away too. There may be a way but I'll have to contact somebody. And . . . we'd need money. Real money. Can you manage that?'

'Probably. If it seems like a good idea.'

He led us through a town that seemed to be dying. There were few people on the streets, the wharves on the river were deserted, the shipyard which had built river boats was now silent, the timberyards and a flour mill seemed empty. The river surface stretched about half a mile to the opposite bank, which was a dark horizon of pine trees. The calm water was almost motionless and Grigor told me, 'The water's always low in late summer. It will freeze over in a few weeks' time.'

He took us to a small house in a side street,

where an old man opened the door and exclaimed with surprise at the sight of him. Grigor introduced us with, 'This is Gyorgi who worked for both my father and me.'

Gyorgi said, 'But we thought — '

'That the Reds had done for me, eh? But listen, Gyorgi: my friends need food and shelter for tonight. Maybe tomorrow night, too. I'm sure they can pay you well, and I'll be making arrangements for all of us to get out of here.'

Gyorgi looked nervously down the street as though expecting to see the Cheka on our trail, but stood back to let us in. Grigor said, 'I'll be back as soon as I can,' and walked off down the street.

He did not return until the next day had faded into the long northern twilight. We'd spent a long boring day in Gyorgi's little house and I was itching with impatience, but I controlled it when he appeared in the company of a hefty old man whose strong smell of fish, and fish scales bespangling his garments, betrayed him as a fisherman. Grigor introduced him as Leonid and said, 'He may be able to help us but first I must ask, do you have any experience handling boats?'

Stefan grinned and I feared he might say something that would expose our real story.

I'd fobbed Grigor's questions off with the yarn that we were consular staff trying to find a way home. I gave Stefan a warning glance and said, 'Yes, we've done a bit of that.'

'Well, the Reds allow Leonid to have a boat because he's a fisherman, and produces food, but he's also got another small boat hidden away. Are you interested?'

'Certainly.'

'And you'd take me with you? I hope the Americans in Archangel will help me get back to the States.'

I asked Leonid, 'The boat's big enough for four of us?'

He answered me with the old Russian term of respect, as from a servant to a master. 'Yes, *gospodin*. And in good condition, together with oars and sail.'

'How far is Archangel by water?'

'Almost a thousand versts. Sailing and rowing, and with the current helping you, you should manage it in about ten days.'

I asked him about the presence of Reds on the river and he told me, 'They have the river boats they've taken over and fitted with guns, and some small motor boats and steam launches. But the river is wide and a little further down it breaks in some places into two or three channels, and winds about a good deal. The banks are rough and often forested, with many places to hide. Keep a good lookout and you should have no trouble.'

'What about provisions?'

'I can sell you some dried fish and potatoes, and fishing gear. And there are villages which might sell you something.'

I said, 'It seems the best way for us. What is your price?'

That began another round of the bargaining which had become increasingly boring. Grigor's eyes glistened when he saw the gold pieces I handed over to Leonid. I asked the old fisherman, 'When should we leave?', and he answered, 'Sunrise. That's when the fishing boats go out and you're not so likely to be noticed.'

I'd no idea what Ana made of all this. As we walked through the quiet streets to Leonid's boathouse I asked her, as I had done often before, 'Are you all right?', and, as often before, she did not answer.

Leonid's yard on the river bank was characteristic of fishermen the world over, with nets drying on lines and sails and oars and baskets scattered around. A burly young man working in a boat at the water's edge, did not even look up at us when Leonid gestured towards him and grunted, 'My son.'

His illegal boat, tucked away in the

boathouse under a tarpaulin, was in reasonable condition and would hold the four of us. We were preparing it for our journey when Leonid held up his hand and we heard the chugging of a motor-boat engine. As it came closer he said, 'Red patrol,' and gestured for us to crouch down in the back of the boathouse while he stood in the entrance. The engine sound came closer then faded into neutral, and we heard raised voices as the Reds chatted, in amiable tones, with fishermen already afloat or about to push off. One shouted, 'Hey, Leonid! You still asleep?'

He waved to them from the entrance, replying, 'Overslept, that's all.'

The Reds exchanged a few more words before they revved their engine up again and motored away. Leonid grumbled, 'What made them come around so early? Usually they're much later.'

He looked as though he'd like to cancel our arrangement but I daresay the weight of sovereigns in his pocket made him change his mind. When we were ready to go he said, 'Keep close to Boris and me until we're in the middle of the river, then go on your own. The patrol's heading upriver now, so with any luck . . . '

We helped Ana into the boat, and stowed our few possessions, and Grigor climbed clumsily aboard. There was no longer any point in Stefan and me concealing our ability to handle a boat and, when Leonid and Boris shoved off, we shipped oars and rowed steadily after them. There were several other fishing boats, under oars or sail, strung along the middle of the river. No doubt they would have noticed an extra boat on the water, especially when Boris and Leonid stopped and began casting their lines and we continued rowing across the river, but they didn't seem to take any notice. Many people, in those days, thought it best to mind their own business and look the other way.

Grigor said nothing until we were approaching the opposite shore. Then he asked, 'Where did you two learn to handle a boat like this?'

I told him, 'Simply by taking seaside holidays. Don't worry about it.'

14

The dark mass of the pines came steadily closer and we almost lost sight of the fishing boats. There was a slight breeze and I decided to take a chance on hoisting the sail. Stefan and I rigged the mast and hoisted the foresail and mainsail, which were made of stained and patched old canvas that seemed unlikely to stand out against the pines. We worked well and quickly together in a way that seemed natural to us, and we were rewarded when the breeze strengthened a little and there was an encouraging ripple of water under the bows. Grigor, watching every move until we had the boat under way with me at the tiller and Stefan handling the lines, said, 'You guys really know what you're doing. You must be navy or something, right?'

We didn't answer that and he shrugged and muttered something. I checked on Ana, sitting up in the bows where we'd positioned her when we left Kotlas. Years later I asked her if she remembered anything of that time and she answered, 'Sort of dimly, yes. I think I understood people were taking me somewhere because something had happened to my family, and that I could trust them. I was still full of aches and pains, but I think I knew I had to endure them until we got to . . . well, wherever we were going.'

I steered close into the western bank and we settled into a steady progress. We kept a good lookout for Reds ashore or afloat but the region seemed deserted. The unchanging forest rolled monotonously past and after a while I felt my eyes closing. I jerked myself awake and saw the others were actually asleep. The calm day and quiet progress were soothing us into relaxation after the tensions of the past weeks. I managed to keep awake for an hour or so and then steered into the bank, so we could climb out and stretch our legs, have a snack and adjust to this new way of travel.

That night we camped on the river bank and set off again very early, and began to teach Grigor something about rowing and sailing. We kept a sharp lookout for Red patrols but saw nothing except, in the far distance, a streamer of smoke from the funnel of a river boat.

Sometime late in the afternoon we began to pass an area where countless tree stumps showed the forest had been exploited. Grigor said, 'There must be a timber camp somewhere,' and we soon came to a few log houses a little way in from the bank. Rough slipways showed where tree trunks had been rolled down into the river, to be drifted or towed to Kotlas or Archangel. A short jetty had served visiting river boats and a huge heap of scrap timber had provided them with fuel.

I was wary of stopping there but we soon found the camp was deserted. Grigor said, 'I reckon nobody's been here since last summer. Probably they never reopened after this season's thaw.'

I decided to stay the night but had the boat hauled close under the bank, about fifty yards up from the camp, with mast and sails lowered and some branches heaped overall for concealment. We made a fire to cook some food but put it out when we'd eaten. We soon found the bunkhouses had hungry populations of lice and fleas but the weather was warm enough for us to sleep outside, and some instinct made me choose a campsite amongst the tree stumps some way from the buildings.

I was glad I'd done so when a strange rhythmic sound awoke me soon after dawn. I peered through the stumps and saw a river boat not far off shore. She was a stern-wheeler, and the rhythmic sound was that of the paddle wheel turning just steadily enough to hold her against the current. Woodsmoke drifted from the funnel and the red flag of the Bolsheviks hung motionless in the morning calm. Ingrained habit made me study the steamer carefully, noting the snouts of machine-guns at various points on the upperworks and the 75-mm French artillery piece, no doubt one of those donated to the incompetent Russian supply service, secured on the foredeck. I'd heard these guns had minimal recoil, perhaps suitable for use on shipboard.

Grigor and Stefan were both awake and they'd crawled up beside me. Stefan asked, 'What d'you reckon they're after?' and I replied 'God knows. Maybe just going to take on fuel.'

Then I saw a man step out of the wheel house on to the upper deck. He looked somehow familiar but he was just too far away for us to make out his features. He carried a speaking trumpet, and after looking round for a few moments he raised it and shouted, 'Hullo! Anyone hearing me forward and make yourself known!'

He began to repeat this call just as I said, 'Hell — that's Iurovsky!', and then, 'Where's Ana?'

Stefan said, 'She was bedded down behind that big stump,' and I told him, 'Quick

— make sure she doesn't stand up.'

He wriggled off while Iurovsky repeated his message two or three times, adding the words, 'Come forward and you'll come to no harm,' which made Grigor snort in disbelief. He asked, 'Who's he after? Is it you guys?'

I didn't answer that, but watched Iurovsky as he went back into the wheelhouse. I hoped the steamboat would start backing out, but a minute or so later a bunch of men tumbled up from the lower decks and assembled round the 75-mm gun. Their leader snapped out the orders but I couldn't understand what they were aiming at until he shouted, 'Fire!'

The stunning detonation of the gun, the screech of the shell and its explosion against one of the log houses, seemed simultaneous. It was repeated almost immediately and Grigor complained, 'Christ — why are they doing that?'

The only answer I could think of was, 'To drive out anyone inside, I suppose.'

Wood fragments flew everywhere as another shell hit. They fired about a dozen in all and by the time they'd finished all the log houses were burning furiously. Iurovsky began surveying the area with binoculars and I crouched down behind my stump, wondering what to do if a landing party came ashore. If we moved quickly enough we might beat them into the forest, and hide until —

Grigor muttered, 'They're going,' and I heard the paddle wheel begin threshing vigorously. But we didn't move out of our hiding places until the sound of it had faded down the river. Stefan said, 'At least they're moving on ahead of us, so they must think we've gone down river,' and Grigor asked again, 'But who's he after? They wouldn't go to all that trouble to catch me again, so it must be you guys.'

I told him, 'Don't worry about it. Let's have some breakfast and then get under way again.'

A morning breeze was stirring and we rowed and sailed down river, keeping close to the bank although the vast expanse of the river surface seemed then to be empty. I taught Grigor to fish and when he'd pulled in his first catch he became quite enthusiastic. During the long days we would land a couple of times to cook our fresh or dried fish, plus some potatoes from our diminishing store. Now and again we passed villages of log houses but the occupants ignored us. The only craft on the water seemed to be fishing boats.

But I still expected to run across Iurovsky again. The determination he'd shown, by getting himself to Kotlas so soon after us, seemed to indicate he was unlikely to give up. I couldn't understand why he hadn't led a search party ashore at the timber camp but thought perhaps the commander of the river boat was in a hurry to get on with other duties.

Long stretches of birch forest, or a kind of heath, began to replace the pines as we travelled northwards. We sailed through channels between scattered islands, and across the mouths of tributaries feeding the great river, and saw no one apart from fishermen. The river boats were evident only as distant drifts of smoke, though we once had a bad fright when a big motor boat came roaring out of an inlet. But the occupants, whoever they were, took no notice of us.

Day followed day without problems except those of choosing the best channel from those in which the river divided itself. Late one evening we found a channel petering out in a wilderness of reeds and had to camp on a dried mudbank. Next morning, which was very fine and clear, we were paddling back to the main stream when we felt a kind of vibration in the air. Grigor asked, 'Thunder? Can't be on a day like this.'

The vibration came again, in a long quivering tremor, and Stefan and I said simultaneously, 'Gunfire!'

I added, 'Artillery, maybe. Perhaps it's around Archangel.'

We heard no more as we made our way back to the river. A great many birds lived amongst the reeds, including geese preparing for their winter migration. One of them, a fine big bird, exploded into the air from directly under the bows of the boat, and to Grigor's own astonishment he reached out and grabbed it. There was an explosion of squawks, hisses and feathers before he contrived to wring its neck. He spent the day plucking and gutting the bird, preparing for the feast we enjoyed that night. The bird was big enough for us to snack on for a couple of days.

At last we entered the delta of the North Dvina River, where it splits into three broad waterways. Each is several miles across when it reaches the sea. Our problem was to choose the one on which Archangel stands, and eventually sail across it to reach the seaport. Increasing river traffic, spotted as distant trails of smoke, helped us choose the right arm, but is so wide that sailing across it was more like seafaring than river boating. A brisk north-easterly breeze whipped the surface into choppy waves and sent cold spray spattering over us but kept the boat bucking along. Grigor and Ana were both seasick and lay huddled in the bottom of the boat.

We were about halfway across when Stefan said, 'Smoke upriver.' We could just see the top of a funnel, emitting a wisp of smoke, over towards the eastern shore. It grew steadily nearer, until we could see it was a tugboat. It was fussing along with a barge towing astern, on a course heading straight for us. We adjusted helm and sails with the aim of passing astern of the barge.

The low-lying eastern shore was well in sight by the time we could see the barge was crowded with Red Army men, and Stefan chuckled, 'Look at the poor bastards hanging over the sides. Most of 'em are spewing their guts up.'

The tug's blunt bows thumped into the choppy waves, sending sheets of spray over the miserable passengers. I saw steam jet from the tug's siren, and heard it screeching, and a man on the upper deck began wig-wagging a semaphore message. We couldn't make anything of it and Stefan said, 'He's probably only telling us to heave to and surrender to the glorious Red Army.'

We were passing well astern when half a dozen bullet holes appeared in the sail, and another bullet tore a splinter from the mast. We couldn't decide whether they were warning shots or fired out of sheer bloody-mindedness, but in any case we were soon out of range. Grigor, roused out of his torpor of seasickness by our talk and manoeuvring, had witnessed the last few minutes of this encounter and he said, 'I'll bet the Reds have a base upriver at Plesinsk. They'll be sending men down to Archangel from there.'

I decided we'd make for the eastern shore, find a snug spot for the night, and hope to complete the journey to Archangel on the following day. We were moving along at a good rate when we saw smoke approaching from the south. Soon we made out the hull of a paddle steamer, with a cloud of smoke above it. When she came closer we saw the smoke was gushing out of the stub of a funnel, poking up out of the wreckage on the upper deck. Other damage showed the Allies had used her as a target but her paddle wheels were unharmed. If any of her crew noticed us they were too busy to worry about us. I found her appearance encouraging, as proof that friendly forces were giving the Reds bloody noses.

The eastern shore provided us with the entrance to a small inlet, well hidden behind clumps of pine and birch. We spent a peaceful night there and awoke to find that gunfire had started early, banging away in ranging shots and then in battery fire. Of course we couldn't tell whether the firing came from Reds or Allies or where they were located.

We moved cautiously down river, keeping fairly close to the bank. After a while the artillery fire stopped and was replaced by that of rifles and machine-guns. When that also faded away we couldn't tell which side had won or lost or whether there'd been an unspoken agreement to take a rest.

I was more interested in the distant sound of what I thought to be an Allied aircraft. I thought it might spot us and we'd somehow be able to indicate we needed assistance. But I couldn't see one in the clear sky and, as the sound came steadily closer, I realized it came from a motor boat speeding upriver. Stefan asked, 'Could that be a Skimmer?', and I answered, 'Looks like it.'

'Skimmer' was the popular name for what were officially known as Coastal Motor Boats, developed by the Royal Navy in 1918 for hit-and-run attacks on German ships and bases. CMBs were two-man torpedo boats, up to fifty-five feet long, with 500 horsepower engines giving top speeds of forty knots. They were known as 'Skimmers' because at top speed, they seemed hardly to touch the water as they raced over it.

This one, presumably on patrol out of

Archangel, slowed down and turned back before it came much closer. If the crew spotted us they probably thought we were local fishermen, but a sight of their boat gave me a spurt of optimism. The navy would have had to ship the CMB to Russia as deck cargo, a laborious business that somehow seemed evidence of the strength of the invasion force.

We plugged along down river, helped by the current, a mild breeze and our own efforts with the oars. I was impatient to end the journey, not least because we'd almost exhausted our scanty supplies.

We'd been moving for another hour or so when Grigor said, 'Smoke back there,' and pointed astern. The funnel and upperworks of a river boat seemed to pop up above the horizon and a few minutes later we could make out the hull. She made steady progress towards us, and I'd just spotted the dot of colour which was the red flag at her masthead when Stefan said, 'Tell you what — I reckon she's a sternwheeler, same as old Iurovsky was fooling around on.'

I turned our boat towards the river bank. It seemed wiser to look for cover before the newcomer became curious, whether Iurovsky was on board her or not. But a keen-eyed lookout must have spotted us and a few minutes later I saw the flash of the gun on her foredeck. Several seconds passed before I heard the flat detonation of the shot shudder over the water, almost in the same instant as a shell splashed down some distance away. I guessed it was intended as a warning shot, telling us to heave to and wait.

By that time the shore was only a couple of hundred yards away. I determined to keep heading for it, while I became conscious of the distant insect-like buzz of the Skimmer's engine. My mind registered that it might be returning while I tried to choose a spot to beach the boat and hop out of it into the cover of the trees.

Another shot from the river boat howled overhead and churned up the water well away from us. A couple more came no closer. Perhaps it was difficult to aim and fire at such a small target as we were. Part of my mind sent a silent message to the river boat skipper: You bloody fool, all that firing's likely to attract the Skimmer.

If he heard me he took no notice. Several more shots followed, perhaps as a reflection of Iurovsky's determination to stop and examine everything on the water — always presuming Iurovsky was aboard the river boat. But they all missed, and we'd almost reached the shelter of the bank when Stefan said, 'Gee, look at that Skimmer move!'

The sound of its approach swelled like that of a diving aircraft. Someone on the river boat decided he could reach us with a machine-gun and a line of venomous jets sprang out of the water, luckily well clear of us. I found myself visualizing a kind of triangular picture in which the river boat was in one angle, we were in another and the Skimmer was in the third — and rapidly changing the shape of the pattern.

Suddenly the river boat skipper realized the Skimmer was a danger coming closer every second. We had a good view of the river boat turning ponderously towards her enemy, with the paddle wheel threshing away under the stern and every gun on board firing at the CMB. But the boat had reached maximum speed and was jinking erratically, hydroplaning along with bows out of the water and white wake churning behind.

The Skimmer was about half a mile from the river boat when it slowed and steadied momentarily and we saw the torpedo leap from its bows. The torpedo had been set for shallow depth running and we saw its sleek sides glisten like a dolphin's as it ran over and under the river surface.

The river boat skipper had a minute or so in which to take evasive action but he was no doubt unfamiliar with torpedoes. He seemed to hesitate, and then to turn broadside on to the approaching weapon as though he hoped to get out of its way.

A torpedo then carried about a quarter-ton of high explosive. The river boats were built with broad, shallow, metal hulls, for use in almost every kind of river conditions, with high superstructures of comparatively light construction because the vessels did not have to face the heavy weather of the open sea. When the torpedo hit the river boat, the outcome was catastrophic. The boat seemed to explode from underneath, with fire bursting up out of the stokehold and adding to the destruction. Smoke, steam, shattered timber and twisted metal, whole or partial human bodies and a mass of burning debris erupted volcanically from the surface of the river and rained hissing back into the water. Fortunately we were well outside the radius of the explosion but we were so overwhelmed by it we hardly noticed the Skimmer turning away and heading back to base. Perhaps its two-man crew hadn't bothered to work out why the Reds had been firing on us and were satisfied with their own achievement.

My confused thoughts quickly became focused on Ana's sudden terrible outburst of sobbing and wailing, while she convulsed as rigidly as an epileptic. I couldn't think what to do except scramble forward and hold on to her, for fear she would hurt herself. She turned and clung to me, shuddering and jerking and uttering those heartbroken sobs and wails. I guessed the explosion shocked them out of her.

Oddly, we three men had virtually ignored Ana during the journey. Grigor gave up attempts to talk to her while Stefan and I simply made sure she had something to eat, somewhere to sleep at night, and someone to ensure she didn't wander too far away when we landed in the daytime. Now, the other two politely looked away while I soothed her, and she gradually relaxed, and eventually, in her usual way, turned away and ignored us.

We got under way again and moved cautiously along until late afternoon. We heard another outburst of shelling and rifle fire from further inland but had no way of guessing who'd come out best. Then the moment came when a couple of soldiers stepped warily out of the undergrowth and down on to a muddy little beach. Even at a distance we could see they weren't Red Army men. They wore British style steel helmets, of British colour and pattern, neatly wound puttees and well-kept webbing equipment. They held their Lee-Enfield rifles in the 'port arms' position as we approached.

Soon I saw that one of them wore corporal's chevrons. He watched as we made for the little beach and as the boat's bows grounded softly in the mud I could see their cap and collar badges. Stefan said, 'Blimey — they're Royal Marines.'

15

The two men of the Royal Marines Light Infantry stared disbelievingly when I spoke to them in English and said, 'I'm Lieutenant Knyve, Royal Navy, and this is Leading Seaman Carter. The lady is my wife and the other man is a refugee.'

The corporal's gaze moved slowly over my soiled and shabby clothing and unshaven face and he studied Stefan in the same way. Then he looked at Grigor who smiled cheerfully back at him and at Ana who ignored him. He asked me, 'you reckon you're a RN lieutenant?'

'That's right. Detached, on special duties.'

Grigor piped up with, 'I always knew they were something like that.' The corporal told me, 'Our unit's back in the woods. We were just seeing there weren't no Reds between us and the river. You'd better come and see our officer.'

He hesitated, then added, 'Sir.'

We followed him a couple of hundred yards into the trees, where a platoon of Royal Marines stood around a fire brewing tea. Their officer watched as the corporal led us towards him, at first without much interest and then, as we came closer, with sudden astonishment. He said, 'Good God! Where the hell did you spring from?'

I recognized him as Lieutenant the Hon. Edric Robbins-Rawlins, who had served with me in the battlecruiser *Imperious* at the Battle of Jutland. He was commonly known as Raffles the Gentleman Burglar, after the popular fictional character of that time and in recognition of some wartime exploit. I addressed him with, 'Hallo, Raffles. What ship are you in nowadays?'

He drawled, 'Ship be damned. I'm a member of the Allied expeditionary force sent here to teach the Bolshies the error of their ways.'

I said, 'I thought the Yanks were in Archangel.'

'So they are. Us too. And a few other odds and ends. Serbs and Italians and God knows what else.'

Despite his scoffing tone he studied us carefully, especially Ana. By that time the clothes she had worn since we left Perm were in a sorry state. The hat she wore crammed down over her head, and the veil attached to it, looked especially unkempt. When we walked from the boat to the RMLI platoon I noticed she had developed a kind of twisting limp, perhaps from the effect of her uncomfortable boat journey on her injuries. I had taken her arm and she had allowed me to help her along, and I had felt a strange mixture of emotions.

Raffles stared at her for a few moments, and then drawled, 'Who's the . . . er . . . lady?'

His tone annoyed me and I snapped, 'My wife!'

'Oh! Ah! I beg her pardon! Wouldn't she like to . . . er . . . sit down? Have a cup of tea?'

He glanced at one of his men, who prepared a tin cup of tea while I helped Ana to sit down. Everyone tried awkwardly not to look at her when she raised the veil a little to sip at the tea.

I told Raffles, 'I've been on special duty in Russia and I shouldn't tell you about it. I think I'd better talk to a senior officer.'

He produced a cigarette case and offered me a Churchman's cigarette, which tasted good after the *papyrossi*. As we smoked he said, 'You'd better see my company commander, but it's a fair walk back to him. Would your wife be up to it?'

We decided Ana should return to the boat with me and Stefan, and we'd carry on down river to the British positions. Grigor would

149

accompany the RMLI platoon on their return journey and then try to persuade the Americans to accept him as a refugee. He said confidently, 'They're sure to need interpreters,' and then bade us a vociferous farewell, 'We'll meet again! You bet! Thanks for everything! Love to your missus!'

Raffles and his men watched as Stefan and I helped Ana to her feet, and I could imagine the gossip which would circulate about 'Ben Knyve's Russian wife'. She was trembling, but I couldn't tell whether this was the result of illness or emotion or the fact that the brief northern autumn was setting in, turning the birch trees golden and the nights cold. Stefan and I half-carried her back to the boat and she gave occasional little gasps of pain but said nothing. We made her as comfortable as we could in the bottom of the boat, folding the mainsail as a bed and covering her with the foresail, and she lay there motionless.

Stefan had begged some Woodbine cigarettes from one of the Marines and I accepted one gratefully. We smoked for a couple of minutes before he asked, 'D'you reckon Ana really understands what's going on? Or about what's happened to her?'

'God knows. I suppose she might be suffering from what the army calls shellshock.

When a man can't take any more he — well, loses his mind.'

'But would she get better?'

'I can't tell you. Don't know enough about it. Anyway, Ana may not be as bad as all that. She may be a lot better when we can get her out of Russia and away from the war.'

We settled down for the usual uncomfortable night and started down river again early next morning. I'd decided to look for a more senior officer than Raffles' company commander and we eventually reached a spot where British soldiers were unloading a barge that had brought supplies up from Archangel. They passed me up the chain of command until an adjutant took me to a lieutenant-colonel: a small man with a piecing pale-grey stare and a posture so rigid he seemed in danger of falling backwards. I feared he might be a narrow-minded martinet but he listened intently to my condensed version of events. I told him Stefan and I had been sent on a secret and confidential mission to the White Russian command, which made him ask, 'Why did they choose a couple of youngsters for a job like that?'

'We have Russian mothers, sir, and mine is . . . well, connected to White Russian aristocracy. And we speak Russian fluently.'

'Ah. Go on.'

151

He raised his eyebrows when I remarked, almost casually, that I had got married and that my wife had been badly injured in a Bolshevik attack. But quick marriages had become customary in wartime and he made no comment.

When I'd finished he said, 'You and your . . . er . . . accomplice will have to go down to Archangel and report to the Senior British Naval Officer. No doubt he'll tell you what to do. You'd better stay here overnight and go down in the barge next morning.'

He gave the orders which resulted in Ana being carried up from the boat in a stretcher and put in the care of an army doctor. When I talked to him later he looked at me queerly as he said, 'There's nothing much wrong with her at the moment except for fatigue, or a minor infection perhaps, but what on earth happened to her? She looks as though she was run over by a tank.'

I said lamely, 'We were caught up in a Red attack.'

'I see. Well, we can look after her tonight but you must make sure she's properly cared for in Archangel.'

Next morning she was helped on to the barge in company with some of the wounded from a British attack on the Reds. A steam tug towed the barge down to Archangel with our little boat bobbing astern.

The doctor had given me a note to the major in charge of the RAMC hospital camp at Archangel and my approach to him, followed by that to Captain Garnett, the Senior British Naval Officer, began two days of interviews in which I had to offer polite refusals to a good many of the questions. But the hospital camp wasn't very busy, and the nurses attached to it accepted Ana with horrified clucks at the condition of her clothing.

Captain Garnett allowed me to send a radio message to Captain Blaze at the Admiralty. This was a complex matter in those days because the low-powered spark transmitters could not communicate directly with London and the operators had to spend time contacting ships that could relay the message, through other ships, to the Admiralty radio station.

My coded message said simply: 'Arrived archangel with one family member please instruct re further movements.' The reply, three days later, told Garnett to 'Expedite return UK Knyve Carter and family member advise ETA soonest.'

When Garnett showed it to me he said sniffily, 'I despise all this secret service business. Not at all suitable for officers of the

Royal Navy. If they want spies they should employ civilians.'

But, by good fortune, he was acquainted with my father and he simplified the acceptance of Stefan and me into the navy's shore base, located in a ramshackle collection of huts and workshops taken over from the Russian navy. The RN officers had adapted one of these as a wardroom and I was sitting there, browsing through some month-old newspapers recently arrived from Britain, when I saw the headline, 'Reds Claim Return of Gold Banked by Nicholas.'

The story, from 'Emery Porteous, our Moslow correspondent', said that, in 1914, Nicholas Romanov had deposited twenty million gold roubles in the Bank of England. His story was that the money was to stand surety for Russian orders of war material from Britain, but the Reds said that was absurd. The value of the war materials had vastly exceeded that amount. They claimed the real reason for the deposit was to support the Romanovs if they were ever forced to flee to England.

The Soviet of People's Commissaries now laid claim to the money. They said that, although it was allegedly paid out of the Romanovs' personal fortune, it really belonged to the people of Russia. But the Bank of England refused to answer the claim, saying that the affairs of depositors were confidential and could only be revealed to legal heirs and successors.

The story concluded, 'The Reds executed Nicholas in July but the fate of his family is still unknown. Rumour says they may be held to ransom against the fortune held in London.'

I supposed that, if the story was true, then Ana might be the sole inheritor of the royal fortune. But I soon had other things to think about, when Garnett told me that the three of us could take passage to England in the troopship *Heroic*, due to leave in three days' time.

A brisk young captain of the RAMC accompanied Ana in the ambulance which brought her to the wharf, where a boat was to take us out to the *Heroic*. He seemed eager to talk about Ana and said, 'It's a miracle she's still alive. She's had enough injuries to kill a frontline soldier. Was it a shellburst or something?'

I nodded, answering 'Yes' without going into details.

He covered much the same ground as Dr Stasanowski but emphasized the muscle damage, saying, 'There are new techniques to deal with it I don't know much about. The

Americans call it physiotherapy. And there's a couple of bones that should be broken again and reset, or they'll cause trouble later on.'

Then he told me, 'The face is really in bad shape. The nose was broken, and the cheekbones, and they haven't set well. Same applies to the jaw, which is now out of alignment . . . to say nothing about the teeth. There's a depressed fracture of the frontal sinus and minor fractures of the floors of the orbits — the eye-sockets, that is — and I think there's an entrapment of the nerve in the right orbit. Must be causing her some pain. And there's the flesh wounds to the face, which have healed but — '

I interrupted with, 'For God's sake! Can't anything be done for her?'

'Oh yes, I expect so. What they now call plastic surgery has taken great steps during the war. So many poor devils have had their faces smashed up. There's a clinic at Aldershot where Harold Gillies and Archie McIndoe have dealt with thousands of them, and I'm sure they — or others — could help Ana.'

I asked awkwardly, 'You've noticed she doesn't say anything?'

'Yes, of course.'

'Do you think there's brain damage?'

'I doubt it. It's obvious she hears what one

156

says, and responds to it — and understands some English, too. Ask her to lift her arm, for example, and she does.'

'What do you think, then?'

'Well, that's something else we've learned about during the war — the psychic damage caused by almost unendurable experiences. There are people who specialize in dealing with that, also, but she may gradually return to normal.'

I digested that, then asked, 'So Ana's dumbness may be mental rather than physical?'

He nodded, then had to step aside because a launch had begun to ferry passengers out to the troopship and a mumber of them pushed past him. Ana and Stefan stood politely waiting for us to finish our conversation. The nurses had contrived quite a respectable new outfit for her, including a hat with a veil which had a slightly flirtatious appearance.

The young doctor continued, 'I'm not a psychologist, as we're beginning to call them, but I would suggest Ana's lack of speech is a kind of withdrawal from other human beings, because they're the cause of her suffering.'

'Is there a cure, then?'

'Time, perhaps. Or simple kindness and patience. And we mustn't forget the physical possibilities. A stroke, perhaps, caused by stress and physical trauma. Or it could be an aneurysm, or even a brain tumour. When you get to England they'll check up on everything like that.'

With these cheerful words he tossed me a salute, and gave Ana a smile, and climbed back into the ambulance. We took our places in a queue and were soon climbing down into the launch. Stefan helped Ana down and I was surprised by his expression, which seemed almost one of tenderness — and by the sudden stab of resentment it sent through me. It was the first time I'd seen him show anything but dutiful attention towards her.

There was plenty of room aboard the *Heroic* and the Merchant Navy doctor arranged for Ana to have a cabin near those occupied by his two nursing sisters. I was hoping for a fairly speedy trip to Liverpool but the homeward-bound convoy ran into a typical Arctic Ocean gale. Black clouds raced overhead at masthead height, the air between sea and sky became a liquid mass of rain and spray driven by a screaming wind, and the sea built up into huge ridges of grey water thundering menacingly towards us. Each of them seemed about to overwhelm the convoy but the ships climbed stubbornly up to the crests, gave us a glimpse over the shrieking wilderness of ocean, and slid down into the valleys again.

I went to see Ana a couple of times but the nursing sisters, a couple of hard-bitten seafaring ladies, allowed me no more than a glimpse of her. They said firmly, 'Leave her to us. We'll take good care of her,' and they certainly plied her with kindness and patience. When the weather improved they took her for walks on deck, talked chirpily to her as she limped between them, and helped her up and down the ship's steps and stairs because she had difficulty climbing them.

One of them, Sister Parminter, spoke to me about her in a slightly accusing tone as though I was the cause of her problems. 'She'll need a lot of care, you know. Can you provide that?'

'Yes, I think so.'

'You can tell she's a very well-brought-up young lady. One of those Russian aristocrats, is she?'

'You could say that.'

'I thought so, She's so dainty and delicate, for all she's been through.'

'How do you think she'll . . . get on?'

She looked consideringly at me. I've found that most nursing sisters, despite frequent exposure to the disasters of life, are incurable romantics, and she confirmed this when she said, 'Just be a loving husband. That's what the poor little thing needs most.'

There were no radio news bulletins in those days but the *Heroic*'s wireless operators picked up scraps of information from other ships and we learned the Allies were at last defeating the Germans on the Western Front and we had a peaceful voyage home. Captain Blaze was waiting on the dockside when the ship berthed in Liverpool and he helped us through the bureaucratic barriers to landing in wartime England, then took us to a hotel where the staff looked snootily at our travel-worn clothing. For the rest of that day he drew our story out of us, making copious notes, and even tried to question Ana but with no more success than anyone else. Heaven knows what she made of everything.

Eventually I gave him what was left of our golden sovereigns plus the pouch of jewels Maria had extracted from Ana's clothing. He looked at them and exclaimed, 'Good God! Well, these should ensure the future of the Grand Duchess Anastasia in our country.'

He handed me an envelope, saying, 'We think it's best if you all go home to Fowlers Haven until we decide what to do next. There's train tickets and some money in there. Simply maintain the fiction that Ana is a girl you met and married. There've been enough five-minute courtships in this war, goodness knows.'

I couldn't imagine my mother believing that story but I took the envelope and said, 'Yes, sir.'

Next day we made the complicated railway journey which carried us into Norfolk and the nearest railway station to Fowlers Haven. I'd telegraphed for a taxicab to meet us and it was at the station, driven by a man whom I'd known since childhood. His expression was so downcast he could hardly give me a smile of welcome, and although sad faces and mourning clothes were common in 1918 England, I asked, 'What's wrong, Mr Simpson? Aren't you glad to see us?'

For a moment he stared blankly, then burst out with, 'Oh, Mr Benjamin, haven't you heard, then? Your blessed mother died yesterday, from that awful influenza, and she'd only been ill for a day or two.'

16

Even in Russia we'd heard about the influenza epidemic sweeping the world, killing millions with the pneumonia which was then virtually incurable, but with youthful insouciance we'd never imagined it affecting us. Mr Simpson rambled on about it during the drive to Knyve's Edge, and when we arrived I tried to get Ana out of the taxi, and into the house, before he overheard any questions about her. But my eldest sister, Natasha, appeared in the doorway first and in her usual big-sister style she demanded, 'Where on earth have you been? Why aren't you in uniform? And whoever's that with you?'

'This is Anastasia. My . . . er . . . wife.'

'Your *wife*! I don't believe it!'

Our confrontation was interrupted by the appearance of Mr Reg Stott, labouring up the steep drive on his official bicycle. Together with his wife and daughter he operated the Fowlers Haven post office and telephone exchange, and the three of them also acted as collectors and disseminators of local gossip. As soon as he saw us he called out, 'Oh, Miz Tasha! Master Ben! 'Tis terrible sad news for 'ee!'

He produced an orange telegram envelope from his belt pouch and handed it to me. I tore it open and found the telegram was from the Admiralty, saying, 'Deeply regret inform you Malta HQ advises Vice-Admiral Sir Lancelot Knyve died yesterday natural causes.' We heard later he suffered a heart attack when he received the telegram telling of his wife's death.

Natasha grabbed the telegram from me, scanned it as though she didn't believe I'd read it properly, then shouted several words which made Mr Stott look at her in shocked surprise. Then she burst into a mixture of tears and prayers. Our mother always said that Natasha was the most Russian of her children.

My second sister, Tatiana, emerged from the house asking 'What's the matter?' and burst into loud wails when she heard the news. I protested, 'Look, girls, Mum and Dad would have hated you going on like this,' and Natasha yelled, 'Mind your own business!'

I paid off Mr Simpson while Mr Stott cycled away, agog with fresh morsels of gossip for the community. Stefan said, 'Very sorry for your news. D'you mind if I nip off home now?'

I said, 'No, of course not,' and forgot to remind him not to tell anyone the true story of Ana. I hoped I could rely on his discretion. Somehow the relationship between us had changed since he shot the deserters. Ever since our earliest days I'd been the leader and he the follower but I'd felt the balance subtly altering. And I was unsure about his attitude towards Ana, which seemed to be shifting towards a closer interest.

She had of course witnessed the noisy reunion with my sisters and, as usual, it was impossible to know what she made of it. I'd begun to shepherd her indoors when our housekeeper, Mrs Travers, appeared, followed by a plump little maid. They also burst into tears when they heard the news, but at least they distracted some attention from Ana.

My third sister, Feodorovna, known as Theo, arrived soon after that. The three sisters soon became so involved in funeral arrangements and plans for memorial services that a couple of days passed before they asked any but cursory questions about Ana and about my activities since Stefan and I left England in the summer. When the questioning intensified I shut it off with, 'Stefan and I went to Russia on secret official business but got mixed up in the revolution and Ana was badly wounded. One day I'll tell you all about it.'

In fact my sisters took little notice of Ana, although they were offhandedly kind to her and gave her clothes and other things. They were too busy with the complications following our parents' deaths. Nobody else was much interested. Our house servants and other employees were too well trained to ask personal questions while the war and the epidemic gave local society other things to think about. Natasha wanted me to take Ana to our local doctor but I thought he was too old and bumbling, and I was expecting Blaze's instructions.

I took Ana for walks and rides around the countryside but I don't know what she made of it. The region around Fowlers Haven could seem bleak and lonely. It was a territory of introverted little towns and villages, feature-less farm lands, and marshes interlaced with reedy channels. The sea coast was a frontier of low cliffs, sandhills and beaches, often lashed by wind and rain.

But it was also a land of birds, especially waterbirds. Huge flocks of them nested there on their migrations north or south, or flourished as natives. Perhaps it was the birdlife of Norfolk that prompted our royal family to establish an estate at Sandringham, about twenty from Fowlers Haven.

The war ended on 11 November 1918 but the influenza epidemic continued to flourish. In Fowlers Haven the fatalities included Stefan's father. Of course my sisters and I, and Ana, went to the funeral but Stefan didn't seem to have much to say to us. I was surprised when, a few days later, he approached me with the words, 'Can I speak to you for a few minutes?'

I eyed him a little warily. There was a look in his eye and a tone in his voice which seemed to add up to a silent challenge. But I nodded assent and he asked, 'Heard anything from the navy?'

Of course he really meant: What's happening about you and me and Ana? I could only answer, 'No,' and try to make a joke of it with, 'Maybe they'll let us stay home over Christmas.'

He acknowledged this with a humourless smile, then said, 'Only I've just got myself engaged to marry Doreen Stott.'

That surprised me but I said, 'Well, congratulations. I didn't even know you were walking out with her.'

He continued, 'I thought I might ask for my dad's job. Those two blokes that worked with him won't be coming back from the war.'

'You mean the head gamekeeper's job? But . . . what do you know about it?'

'I picked up plenty when I was a kid. And I know every inch of the Knyve farms and estate, same as you do.'

But I said, 'Hold on. You signed on as a regular, which means you won't be discharged until you're thirty.'

'I know. But you could buy me out. Twelve pounds it would cost you, with the service I've got in.'

Twelve pounds was an appreciable sum in those days. It would pay your chauffeur's wages for a month or buy a handmade suit by a Savile Row tailor. But, as Stefan's news began to sink in, I was less concerned about the money than about Stefan's engagement to Doreen Stott. The Stotts were notorious gossips and I felt certain that, sooner or later, Doreen would wheedle Ana's story out of Stefan. After that it would become public property.

I asked him, 'Are you sure about that?' and he gave me what was almost a pitying smile.

'Certainly. Everyone in the mess decks knows that. And I seen it once in that big book of rules.'

'You mean King's Regulations and Admiralty Instructions?'

'Something like that.'

I said, 'Twelve pounds is a fair amount. Just let me think about it.'

'You can spare twelve quid — and don't think too long. Me and Doreen've got arrangements to make.'

His insolent tone made me understand his strategy. During our time in Russia we'd never discussed the possible consequences to Ana if her true identity became known but Stefan was cute enough to understand that, as legitimate heiress to the throne of Russia, she'd be in danger from the Reds. I also feared the effect sudden publicity might have on her state of mind.

Now Stefan was using his knowledge to secure release from the navy plus a comfortable shore job. If I didn't oblige him he'd make the story public.

But I said only, 'I'll let you know tomorrow,' and he nodded and ambled away.

Of course I knew the situation was impossible. Anything you pay a blackmailer is only the first instalment — and how could I take the risk that he would not, even unintentionally, tell the story to Doreen Stott?

Next morning I took the first step by telephoning Captain Blaze at the Admiralty. There were no automatic exchanges in those days and the call had to go through the

Fowlers Haven exchange, operated by the Stotts, which suited my purpose.

It was pretty cheeky of a junior office to ring up a senior in this way, but when I asked Blaze, 'I wonder if you have any orders for me, sir?' he answered quite amiably, 'Not yet. Just wait a few more days.'

'Yes, sir. And . . . you remember Leading Seaman Carter?'

'Yes, of course.'

'He's asked me to help him buy out of the navy. He wants to marry and get a shore job, which I can provide for him.'

'Ah. Pity to lose a good man like that. All right — write me a letter with details of his service and character and so on, and I'll pass it on with my recommendation. There shouldn't be any problems now the war's over. Must go now. G'bye.'

The phone clicked into silence, followed by more clicks as one or another of the Stotts pulled plugs out of the switchboard.

I let a few hours pass, then sent for Stefan and told him about my call to Blaze. Something in his expression told me he knew about it already, no doubt from one of the Stotts. But he said, respectfully enough, 'Thank you, sir.'

I continued, 'And the job's yours if the navy discharge goes through. In fact we can make a start tomorrow morning, by having a shot at a few rabbits.'

Wartime rationing was still in force, meat was in very short supply, and plump rabbits were very marketable as well as being welcome in our own kitchen.

Stefan duly presented himself next morning, looking the picture of a gamekeeper in his father's boots and breeches, tweed coat and cap, gamebag over one shoulder and a double-barrelled twelve-bore shotgun in the crook of the other arm. I was similarly clad, and each of us had a pocketful of Eley-Kynoch cartridges. The main difference between us was that my shotgun came from Purdey's of London while his was a much cheaper model.

The Knyve's Edge shooting rights covered a considerable area, including the twelve farms rented from the estate and a stretch of Fowlers River. We tramped a good distance and found plenty of bunnies. Stefan was a natural shot but I was out of practice, and he was responsible for most of the rabbits that filled our gamebags. That suited me because it fed his self-satisfaction and he paid little attention to me. Perhaps he didn't even notice I'd led us to Thurlow's Piece, the smallest and most overgrown of the farms and the furthest from the main house,

170

occupied by an old couple who probably made just enough, from poultry and a few dairy cows, to pay the rent and tithes and keep themselves.

The day had started clear and cold but a sea wind had steadily heaped dark clouds from one horizon to another. A cheerless drizzle began to fall and I told Stefan, 'That's enough. Let's head for home.'

Soon we came to the spot I had in mind, where a wooden stile in a thick hedge gave access from one field into another. A stile, which is simply a wooden step between a couple of cross-pieces secured to uprights, is a kind of permanent gate, allowing humans to climb over but barring sheep and cattle. I'd always been taught to unload a shotgun before climbing a stile and I broke my gun open as we approached, but only extracted one of the cartridges and dropped it in my pocket. Stefan, following behind, couldn't have seen whether I extracted one or two.

I heard the clicks behind me as he unloaded his gun, just as I climbed over the stile. When I stepped down on the other side I turned and saw him just swinging his leg over. Our eyes met as I raised my shotgun and I think he understood, in that final second, what was about to happen and why.

17

It was unlikely that Constable Arthur Dobson, the senior of the three constables stationed in the Fowlers Haven area, would question anything said to him by Lieutenant Benjamin Knyve who had so recently become Lord of the Manor of Knyve's Edge. He'd asked me for a statement and copied it laboriously into his notebook, then read it back to me. His voice became solemn as he read the final paragraph: 'I had my back to Stefan when he climbed over the stile and didn't see what happened, but when I heard the shot I turned and saw him fall. His shotgun lay on the ground between us and I presume he dropped it accidentally and that it discharged when the butt hit the ground.'

I yawned as I nodded agreement and he asked me to sign the statement. That day seemed to have been going on for a very long time. After Stefan fell I examined his gun and found he had done everything properly. He had extracted both cartridges before climbing the stile, as a precaution against just such an accident as he had apparently suffered. Like a good gamekeeper he had saved discharged cartridges in one pocket, rather than throwing them away to litter the countryside, and I took out one of these plus an unfired cartridge from the other pocket and slipped them into the shotgun breeches.

Then I ran home across the fields and along the lanes and arrived suitably distressed and breathless. I rang the police station and of course one of the Stotts had to put me through — Mrs Stott on this occasion — and I heard her scream of shock and anguish when she listened in to my report of the death of her daughter's fiancé.

A dreary rain was falling when I returned to the body with our old doctor, Dobson, and two men with a stretcher. Fowlers Haven did not possess such refinements as an ambulance and the doctor drove his model-T Ford along the lanes to a spot as near as possible to the 'accident'. The winter afternoon was fading as we trudged over a field to Stefan's body and the rain glistened in the light of the lantern the doctor used to examine it. When he saw the hideous wound he said cynically 'You didn't need me to certify the poor bugger's dead.'

We took the body to the police station and lodged it in the only cell. The news had spread by that time and the Stotts were among those who had gathered outside, with

Doreen keening hysterically.

Dobson phoned a report to his Norwich headquarters and on the following afternoon I was woken from a nap to be interviewed by a detective inspector and detective sergeant. The DI was a wiry, snappy little terrier of a man and when he began firing questions at me I quickly pulled myself together. Murder was a serious business in those days and if you made a wrong move you might find yourself on the gallows trap with the executioner fitting the noose around your neck.

The DI showed me the cartridges from Stefan's gun in a paper bag and asked, 'Would your fingerprints be on these?'

I said, 'Probably. I opened a new box of cartridges before we left home and shared them between us.'

'Where are the cartridges you said, in your statement, you took out of your gun before climbing the stile?'

Dobson had asked the same question, but only because he was worried in case I'd replaced them in the gun and forgotten to take them out again. I said easily, 'Here,' and produced a couple from my pocket. 'They happen to be the last two I had left yesterday. I'd fired all the others at the bunnies.'

He examined them frowningly but shotgun

cartridges, which fire a load of small shot out of a cardboard tube along a smooth barrel, give little away. He snapped, 'Why didn't Carter extract the cartridges from his gun, like you did, before climbing the stile?'

'I suppose he just didn't bother.'

'Wouldn't he have seen you do it?'

'Of course, but everyone takes chances sometimes.'

'Didn't you remind him?'

'I didn't think of it.'

'But didn't you notice?'

'As I said in my statement, I was ahead of him.'

He opened and closed Stefan's shotgun a couple of times, asking, 'You'd have heard these clicks if he'd opened the gun, to take out the cartridges, wouldn't you? Didn't you notice their absence, warning you he hadn't opened the gun and removed the cartridges?'

'I'm sorry to say I didn't. We'd had a busy afternoon, the weather was turning miserable and I was looking forward to getting home.'

'Have you ever known a shotgun to fire when it's dropped?'

'I don't think I've ever seen one dropped.'

'So how — and why — did Carter drop his?'

'I've no idea. Our guns were wet by that time. Perhaps he let it slip out of his hands.'

The DI placed an open hand on his solar plexus, saying, 'All the shot hit him here. He was too close for it to spread out. Why should it have hit him like that?'

'Pure bad luck, I suppose. It could just as easily have missed him.'

'I'd like to test this gun. Put a cartridge in it and drop it butt first and see what happens.'

I laughed pleasantly. 'You're welcome to try it, but not when I'm there. Who knows which way the muzzle would point?'

He began to question me about my relationship with Stefan and contrived to hint it had a sexual flavour. I expected him to say something like 'Every nice boy loves a sailor' but he didn't go that far.

The navy had taught me to keep my head in a crisis and I answered him calmly and even smilingly. Eventually he abandoned his attempts to label me as the culprit but uttered a warning 'No doubt we'll be talking again' when I ushered him out of the front door. I replied with a polite, 'I suggest you make it soon or I may have gone back to sea,' but I never saw him again.

Of course gun accidents do happen and the inquest returned a verdict of accidental death. We had buried Stefan before that, in the graveyard of the little stone church built by the Normans. Most of the village was there, including of course the Stotts, but there was no sign of blame or suspicion. The attitude towards me was one of sympathy.

I took Ana to the funeral service because I thought it would be a good opportunity for the neighbourhood to have a look at her. People had had glimpses of her when I took her for walks or rides but I'd contrived to avoid direct contacts. Ironically, though, the day of the funeral was that of a North Sea storm, with lashing winds and rains dropping the temperature inside and outside the church. She was so bundled up in one of Natasha's coats and hats that her face was almost hidden.

She sat close to me in the church and something in the music must have struck a chord in her. To my surprise her gloved hand crept into mine, though she did not turn her head to look at me. The feel of her fingers sent a strange warmth coursing through me and I seemed to feel calmer and more confident towards her, as though she was more than a wife in name only.

A few mornings after the funeral I was sorting through a mass of papers forwarded by the family solicitor in Norwich, and gloomily discovering some of life's complications such as death duties and other taxes. I heard a car engine throbbing up the drive and a few minutes later our elderly parlour-maid, Doris, brought me an elegantly engraved visiting card. It said, 'Sir Anthony Kennedy,' and, in very small type, 'Buckingham Palace.'

Doris said, 'The gemmun asks could you very kindly meet him outside,' and I went out to the big boxy Rolls-Royce limousine, its black enamel and nickel plating gleaming with elbow grease. The uniformed chauffeur opened a rear door for me and a genial voice said, 'Lieutenant Knyve? Do please come in.'

The rear compartment was like a luxurious little room, with sound-proof glass separating us from the chauffeur, and what I supposed was a plain-clothes policeman, in the front seat. Sir Anthony was a rubicund smiling man, who said 'Do forgive me for calling on you in this arbitrary fashion, but I'm sure you understand the need for complete confidentiality?'

'Of course.'

Obviously he did not think it necessary to explain why he was there. He asked, 'How is the . . . ah . . . young lady?'

Something made me answer bluntly, 'Sad, lost, lonely, speechless and often in pain. Something must be done soon.'

He said sympathetically, 'Quite. That's why I'm here. If I send this car for you tomorrow could you bring her to Sandringham? Just for a brief visit, you understand?'

'You mean the — '

'Let's just say her first cousin once removed would very much like to see her. I'd prefer not to say anything more just yet.'

I agreed to the arrangements and tried to explain them to Ana, but as usual couldn't tell whether she understood. The Rolls-Royce reappeared at the appointed time, a notable achievement considering the complex of minor roads between Sandringham and Knyve's Edge, and the same chauffeur gravely assisted Ana into the car.

Some people have described Sandringham as ugly and uncomfortable but I paid little attention to our surroundings as Sir Anthony escorted us into the house and then into a study where a fire burned brightly. The man who stood before it had a remarkable likeness to the Emperor Nicholas of Russia. This was understandable because they were both grandsons of Queen Victoria, only a couple of years apart in age, and both of the rather short sturdy build. Their points of resemblance included blue eyes, brown hair and what were then known as 'torpedo' beards and moustaches.

He gave us the beginnings of a welcoming smile as Sir Anthony ushered us towards him, saying, 'Sir, may I present — '

But Ana interrupted him by crying out, 'Papa! Papa!' in a strange cracked voice and then blundering forward to embrace the man standing there.

18

For some time Ana couldn't stop crying. The tears poured out of her as though from a reservoir dammed for months. Sir Anthony helped her to an armchair and she sat there swaying to and fro, wailing loudly and soaking the handkerchiefs provided by three embarrassed males.

I thought the tears were those of disappointment because the man in the study was not her father but simply his double, or something close to it. But she told me later, 'When I thought it was Papa standing there something seemed to go 'Click!' in my head, and I started to remember who I was and some of the terrible things that had happened to my family, and that somehow you brought me out of Russia and all the way to this place.'

When her tears tapered off Sir Anthony rang for a footman, who brought champagne. This gesture, no doubt prearranged, was significant because King George V and his family had sworn off alcohol during the war. Ana accepted a half-glass and seemed to relax as she sipped it with her twisted lips. Then we went into luncheon, a simple meal which I hardly tasted because the two men questioned me so intensely about my Russian experiences. They tried to question Ana but she was too shy to be drawn into the conversation.

Coffee was served in a drawing-room, accompanied only by Sir Anthony. He explained, 'We soon have to catch the train back to London from King's Lynn. We're terribly busy nowadays.'

He sipped coffee, then told me, 'I am to advise you that the palace will cover all medical costs for the Grand Duchess Anastasia. We suggest you contact Lord Borden, of Harley Street, in the first instance, and follow his advice thereafter.'

He bowed to Ana, shook my hand, and said, 'Don't hesitate to contact me at any time. And . . . I'm sure you'll keep all this very confidential. Russian royalty isn't popular in Britain. Many people blame them for the revolution, and the collapse of Russia, and all the problems that caused the Allies. There could be an awful fuss if people knew the palace is helping the Grand Duchess.'

Ana didn't look much like a Grand Duchess on the way home. Huddled in her seat, hat and veil pulled down over her face, she seemed disconnected from the world. But

I had things to say to her and I started by asking, 'Did you understand what Sir Anthony said about keeping things . . . well, secret?'

She answered, 'Of course! Do you think I want the Reds to kill me like they killed my family?'

A bit lamely I said, 'Of course not,' and she asked, 'When can I start the medical treatment they talked about?'

'As soon as I can make an appointment in London.'

She thought that over, then asked hesitantly, 'Is it true about you marrying me? I don't think I remember that.'

'Yes, but it was only to help you escape. I expect it can be annulled, if you wish.'

'You mean like a divorce?'

'Yes, sort of.'

She said primly, 'Divorce is a sin, I've always been told.'

But I changed the subject with, 'Listen, I expect some people in Fowlers Haven will work out we've been to Sandringham. From this car, and so on. It's amazing how quickly stories get round, and might be heard by the wrong people. Understand?'

She answered almost cheekily, 'Then we must make up our own story first!'

'Right! I think we can simply say the King

heard, through the navy, about my visit to Russia and meeting and marrying you. And he invited us to Sandringham to give him first-hand information about conditions in Russia, and you were so excited you got your speech back!'

It was a flimsy enough story but our household accepted it with marvelling exclamations. The same applied to the rest of Fowlers Haven, where people were used to colourful stories brought home by generations of the Knyve family.

But Natasha, who was staying on at Knyve's Edge while my other sisters returned to their families, was so intrigued by this story that she deluged Ana with questions. And after a few days she told me, 'I'm really appalled by the things Ana told me!'

Cautiously I asked, 'Oh? Why's that?'

'Well, she says you bought her from her parents when she was only fifteen. They sold her to get money for food. And you virtually forced her to marry you, then made her go looking for food during a battle so she was badly wounded!'

Thinking quickly, I scoffed, 'That's rubbish. I gave her parents money because they were starving, and they asked me to look after Ana. And our marriage was just a formality, to get her out of Russia.'

'Hmm. But what about the rape?'

'What rape?'

'When a Bolshevik raped her and she was so shocked she lost the power of speech, and you rescued her from him.'

'Well . . . er . . . I think she's a bit confused about that. She was injured in a surprise attack, and lost her memory and her voice.'

But various versions of this story went the rounds and at least helped to obscure the truth. When I asked Ana, 'Why ever did you tell Natasha all that nonsense?', she answered demurely, 'She kept asking questions about you and me, and I can't tell her the truth.'

Soon after that we went to London to see Lord Borden. We put up at Brown's Hotel and went to Harley Street next morning. The examination took a long time and when Borden sent for me I found Ana dressing behind a screen. He was a tall elderly man whose melancholy visage made me expect bad news, but he said, 'Mrs Knyve doesn't want to tell me how she came by her war injuries except that they happened in Russia, but of course that's her privilege. I understand you know about most of the injuries but there may be others. The spleen, for example, is injured and should be removed. But that's reasonably straightforward.'

He steepled his fingers, looking at me in a

185

way which seemed to invite me to ask, 'How about her face?'

'Ah yes. Well, no doubt you've heard about what's becoming known as 'plastic surgery'. I believe the surgeons can effect improvements but it will be a long process.'

Ana finished her dressing and came to sit by me. Lord Borden outlined a programme which, he suggested, could be carried out in the Alberta Hospital, a private establishment where one of the plastic surgeons dealt with non-military cases. When I asked him how long it would take he said, 'I'm no expert in this but I believe it could be several months.'

Ana was very subdued on the way back to the hotel, where I'd taken adjoining rooms. When I opened her door for her she murmured, 'Come in for a minute,' and when we were inside she pushed the door shut and, with a jerky movement, swung round to embrace me. Hugging me tightly she gulped, 'Why did God allow these things to happen to me? I never hurt anyone!'

Of course I couldn't answer that and in any case I was more interested in the feel of her against me. It was a long time since I'd held a female body so closely and my own was vigorously aware of the fact. But she eased away again, saying awkwardly, 'I've never thanked you for taking care of me . . . I'm more grateful than I can tell you.'

After lunch she said she was sleepy and went to her room. I took the opportunity to nip along to the Admiralty. I half-expected Captain Blaze would be too busy to see me, but I was admitted after a brief delay. He seemed to know everything that had happened to Ana and me since we met him in Liverpool. I told him about Ana's impending treatment and he asked, 'But what do you want to do with yourself?'

Almost without thinking I answered, 'Go back to sea.' The routine of shipboard life, with its specific duties and responsibilities, suddenly seemed very attractive.

He said, 'That's easily arranged, but what about Ana? She is your wife, after all, and someone has to be responsible for her.'

I almost said something like, 'I didn't expect to have to look after any of the Romanovs when I got them to England.' But I'd been trained not to argue with superior officers and, to my surprise I found I liked the idea of Ana being my wife. The solution came to me and I said, 'I think my sister Natasha would look after her while I'm away. She was widowed in the war and has no children. She seems to get on all right with Ana and it would be . . . well, a reason to go on living in our family home.'

'Very well. I'll leave it to you to work out, and I'll see what I can do for you.'

Three weeks later, Ana had entered hospital and I had been appointed as the first lieutenant, which meant the second-in-command, of the light cruiser *Spartan*. Such a position usually went to a higher rank and seniority than mine but the *Spartan* was just small enough for me to qualify, and Blaze had provided an important step in my career.

The *Spartan* had just finished refitting in Chatham Dockyard and was in the usual mess of a ship in dockyard hands. Together with a small advance party I had plenty to keep me busy and I was responsible for countless details as the ship prepared for duty.

Dockyard towns have long experience in catering for seafarers' needs and I soon made the acquaintance of a red-haired Irish lady known as Casey. A night with her was a civilized experience because, apart from her handsome fee, she expected dinner and whatever entertainment Chatham might offer before returning to her flat. She was a charming companion but, in the instant of consummation, I was disconcerted when Ana's damaged features flashed into my mind.

On commissioning day our crew marched

from the barracks and stood in long ranks on the quayside, waiting to be ordered aboard. They looked too many to fit into the ship but one of my tasks had been that of assigning each man his space in the mess decks, action station, fire and collision station and so on, and I knew there was room for everyone. Their faces ranged from the fresh pink of boy seamen to the bronzed features of middle-aged petty officers and at one moment I found myself absurdly seeking Stefan's face amongst them.

Our captain, known on the lower decks as Sniffer Skipper because of his habit of giving a loud self-satisfied sniff after issuing an order, donned sword-belt and frock-coat and went ashore to report readiness. The White Ensign, Union Jack and Commissioning Pendant streamed from ensign staff, jackstaff and masthead when we secured to a buoy in the River Medway to take on stores and ammunition. We were hard at work when we received the signal beginning, 'Proceed immediately join Baltic Force — '

I had plenty to keep me busy and might not have given much thought to Ana's surgical treatment if it had not been for our navigating lieutenant. His brother had been wounded in the face in the last days of the war, and he had visited him in the Aldershot clinic founded by Harold Gillies, a pioneer of plastic surgery. He said, 'You never saw anything like some of those poor devils there. One of the things the surgeons do is to attach a skin graft by peeling back a strip of skin from a forearm and stitching it to a wound. That means you have to lie there with your arm fastened to your face until the skin graft grows on.'

I tried to open the subject, conversationally, with our surgeon lieutenant, but he was a chubby extrovert principally interested in bridge, golf, whisky and women. He guffawed, 'Think a plastic surgeon might improve your ugly mug, do you? Hop up on the operating table and I'll see what I can do for you!'

Baltic Force was stationed in the Gulf of Finland to blockade Russian warships, manned by the Reds, in the naval base of Kronstadt, to prevent them slipping out to attack Allied ships and bases. We arrived when the ice was beginning to break up and drift out to the open sea, and great floes banged against the ship's sides. Our tactics were aggressive and we torpedoed two of their ships at anchor, using CMB Skimmers. They responded by launching sea-mines to drift with the winds and tides, and these sank a couple of our cruisers.

Blockade work can be a dreary occupation but it suited me at the time. The familiar routines, and the demands on me for constant attention to detail, prevented me from thinking too much about Ana and plastic surgery.

Natasha was not a prolific correspondent or facile writer and she covered her occasional visits to Ana in such wording as, 'The hospital is a heck of a long way from here and I might as well have saved the time and cost of a visit, because they've got Ana sewn up so that she can't talk properly. But she's alive and kicking and the surgeon seems optimistic.'

Winter turned into spring while the situation in western Russia simmered towards explosion. A White army, despite inefficiency and infighting, was battling towards St Petersburg. The Reds, though demoralized in some areas, were being reorganized by leaders who solved problems with firing squads. Resistance to Bolshevism created the Red Terror, in which hundreds of thousands died and countless refugees fled the country. The Baltic provinces of Finland, Latvia, Estonia and Lithuania, still partly occupied by the German army, were rebelling against the Bolsheviks.

We had a close-up view of this situation in

early summer, when a radio message from HQ ordered us to 'Proceed immediately to position approx five miles south of Amazi on Baltic coast of Estonia to take off party British nationals.'

We were halfway through the twenty-hour run to Amazi when the captain summoned me to the chartroom. Pointing to our destination on the chart, he grumbled, 'What the devil's a party of our people doing there? Anyway, I want you to command the landing party.'

I selected the landing party, of a petty officer, eight seamen with rifles and bayonets, and a signaller, and they stood by as we approached the little port of Amazi on a flawless summer morning. A few small craft were fishing outside the harbour but they made for home when we appeared. Estonians were fighting for their freedom against Bolsheviks, White Russians and the German army, and were understandably wary of strangers.

We cruised down the coast, a monotonous stretch of beach backed by sandhills, until we reached the rendezvous. Four small buildings stood in a gap in the sandhills near a cart-track leading inland.

There wasn't a sign of life until the foremast lookout spotted a group of figures running down the track on to the beach, with another party close behind. There seemed to be some kind of scuffle going on when the captain ordered, 'Landing party away!'

By the time our boat crunched on the firm sand the pursued and pursuers had all vanished into one of the buildings, which were no more than wooden shacks used for holiday houses or fisherman's huts. The mass of footprints in the sand showed where the two parties had scuffled together and led to the shack in which they were concealed.

I divided the party into two, and led one group towards the shack while the others went behind it. I saw a face in a window, and felt very exposed, but thought the guns of the *Spartan*, in full view offshore, would cause any antagonists to think twice about resistance.

The shack door opened and a German officer came out. His coal-scuttle helmet, grey-green uniform, leather equipment and weathered unshaven face all showed the effects of long campaigning. He advanced a few paces, saluted, and introduced himself as, 'Oberleutnant Fromm. You have zigaretten?'

I returned his salute and introduction and offered my cigarette case. He inhaled and exhaled luxuriously as I asked, 'Are you holding British subjects in there?'

'Ja. Six men, four women, three children.'

'Then release them immediately, please.'

'But first we negotiate. Agree?'

I scoffed, 'No! You're surrounded already and I can signal for more men. Give up our people now!'

'But if we resist what will become of them?'

I thought for a moment of drawing my revolver and shooting him, but he must have read my body language because he said smilingly, 'My men already are aiming at you.'

I asked, 'What do you want?'

'Just take us away from here, so we can reach German headquarters in Finland. There's only seven of us, separated from our regiment. We don't want to surrender to Estonians.'

At that moment Sniffer Skipper showed his impatience with a long blast from the ship's siren, sounding ill-tempered even from a good distance away. I told Fromm, 'All right — bring them out,' and he barked orders towards the shack. The second of the hostages to emerge was Emery Porteous, the British journalist I'd said farewell to in Moscow a year ago.

19

I suppose every senior officer or executive believes he can do any job better than his juniors and Sniffer Skipper left me in no doubt that, if only he'd been in command of the landing party, he would quickly have sent the Germans packing. Now we had to go to the trouble and expense of feeding them for a day, adding four hours to the ship's steaming time to land them in Finland, and so on.

But Porteous soothed my abraded ego when he said, 'My God, we were scared of those Jerries. I'm sure they'd have knocked us off if you hadn't done what they wanted, out of sheer bloody-mindedness.'

He told me his group consisted of Britons, some with families, who'd been doing such work in Moscow as representing British firms. 'But we all hung on too long, and in my case the Reds wouldn't allow my paper to send another journalist to take my place. When we tried to get out we found the train services are all cock-eyed. We couldn't get to St Petersburg and ended up on a station in Estonia, with no more trains and a twenty-mile walk to the sea coast.'

I asked, 'But how did the navy know about you?'

'Ah, the story gets even better. We were standing there like lost bloody sheep when this railway worker — not much more than a labourer by the look of him — spoke to us in good English. He said he thought he could get us picked up on the coast, told us where to go and even gave us some money. I reckon he was some kind of a British agent — or a mighty good-hearted Estonian. And then those bloody Germans spotted us and chased us at the last moment.'

He told me he intended to write a book about his experiences in Russia and would like to include me and Stefan. When I asked, 'Whatever for?', he winked and said, 'Well, it's a pretty intriguing story, isn't it? Here you are, an officer in the Royal Navy, but when I first met you and Stefan you were a couple of civilians. Then there was that episode with the Germans in Stockholm, and most of all the time when you bought the prisoners off the firing squad. And now you possibly saved my life.'

I said, 'Well, I suppose I can't stop you. But I'd sooner you didn't piss off the Admiralty by using my real name.'

'OK, then. And what about Stefan?'

'He had an accident. Didn't survive it.'

'Oh. Sorry about that.'

He began to talk about the whole Russian disaster including the fate of the Romanovs. 'The Reds won't admit to murdering the whole family but everyone believes they did — though there's a rumour that the youngest daughter got away.'

Service in the Royal Navy had taught me to keep a straight face under most circumstances and I simply murmured, 'Really?'

Soon after that we landed the British refugees, and the German contingent, in the Finnish port of Helsingfors. The British Military Mission looked after our people but I never heard what happened to the Germans.

We rejoined Baltic Force and were soon in action again. Our ships shelled Red positions resisting the White advance on St Petersburg, sank some Russian ships and lost some of ours to mines or bad weather, and fought off some air attacks. In the end it was all wasted effort. The White offensive collapsed and we had to help with some of the after-effects: the swarms of refugees trying to escape and the typhus epidemic which killed thousands.

We received mail occasionally and in one of Natasha's letters she said, 'I've now seen what the surgeons are doing for Ana and it's remarkable,' but gave no details. She was more expansive on plans for her second marriage, to our friend and neighbour Billy Barron, who'd lost a hand in the war. I'd suggested to Ana she should not write to me, in case a letter somehow went astray and the Reds learned of her survival, but in one of Natasha's letters there was a line saying, 'I am so very grateful for all you have done for me. — A.'

Porteous, as a journalist, was a fast writer, and his publishers rushed his book through to catch the Christmas market. I received a copy in my Christmas mail, with his signature and 'Hope to see you again' on the flyleaf. I found that Stefan and I received mentions under fictitious names and descriptions.

Winter came with searing winds and, by December, our ships were crunching through ice floes. We thought we might be frozen in, but orders to withdraw came on the last day of the year. Allied intervention in the revolution was beginning to fade and Baltic Force soon returned to its bases in England.

A letter from Ana awaited me when the *Spartan* returned to the Medway. It told me she was about to leave hospital and so I presumed she had returned to Knyve's Edge. Otherwise the letter was short and polite, as though she was writing to a stranger. Of course we were strangers in many ways, with no point of contact except that, simply by obeying orders, I had helped to save her life. We'd hardly spoken about that time in Russia and I didn't know how much she remembered about it, or about the murder of her family.

I wondered whether the time had come for me to make a graceful withdrawal. Perhaps a divorce? I'd heard that non-consummation of a marriage could be grounds for divorce, but divorces were still looked down on in polite society — including the Royal Navy. And if we did divorce, who would look after her? Perhaps her British relations, or those of her Russian relations who had escaped the revolution and were living in western Europe. But then the story of her background would almost inevitably emerge, and she might be in danger from the Reds.

Perhaps our marriage wasn't even legal, or not valid in Britain. And, most of all, did she want me for a husband? And did I want her for a wife? I tried to put such things in a letter to her but ended by tearing it up.

When my turn for leave came I sent a telegram to Natasha, asking her to pick me up at the nearest railway station to Fowlers Haven, and set off as dismally as though I was being invalided out of the Navy. When the train arrived Natasha, with her new husband beside her, saw me and waved. A slender girl stood with them; head rather bent so that her hat brim hid her face. When I approached she raised her head and I saw, of course, it was Ana, with a face remarkably changed from the one I'd known. The scars and stitch-marks were still visible, inadequately camouflaged by cosmetics, but the basic features had been restructured and had somehow made her another person.

The blue eyes watched me with a mixture of emotions as strange as those I felt myself, until Natasha asked amusedly, 'Well, Ben, aren't you going to kiss your wife?'

I did so rather clumsily and her lips felt unresponsive against mine, but when we took our seats in the car her hand found mine and clasped it during the drive to Knyve's Edge. When we arrived, Natasha said, 'Oh, by the way, Ben, I'm putting you and Ana in Mummy and Daddy's old room.'

I stammered, 'But — '

She raised her eyebrows. 'What's the matter? You're the lord of the manor now, you know.'

Of course I did know that but the large bedroom, which in the manner of those days had a dressing-room for my father and a boudoir for my mother attached to it, seemed like forbidden territory. My brothers and sisters and I had all been born in the marriage bed but, after infancy, rarely allowed in the bedroom. My mother always slept in the bed but my father often used the single bed in the dressing-room, where he kept all his clothes and toilet gear. My sisters were allowed into the boudoir for feminine discussions and instructions but it was taboo for boys.

But, primarily, I realized Natasha must have accepted the fact of my marriage to Ana. Perhaps she even believed the stories we'd told her. Consequently she thought Ana and I were now entitled to use what had been my parents' quarters. And she had no doubt mentioned the arrangement to Ana, who seemed to have accepted it.

All this passed through my mind in a few seconds, until I managed to gulp, 'Oh yes — thanks — that'll be fine.'

After dinner that evening we all discussed the future of the estate. I didn't want to leave the navy and so would often be absent from home. I explained to Ana that, as a navy wife, she could accompany me to whatever station, at home or overseas, I might be attached to as a seagoing or shore-based officer. Natasha had made the ideal choice of second husband because Billy had trained as an estate agent before going to war. Our own estate agent had left us for a better job during the war, but now Billy could manage the estate and its properties and distribute the income according to our parents' wills. The house was big enough to provide plenty of space for Natasha and Billy and any children they might produce plus Ana and me, and any children, whenever we might choose to live there.

Of course these optimistic discussions couldn't foresee the agricultural depression of the 1920s and the worldwide depression of the 1930s and the total change in lifestyles brought about by the Second World War and its sequels.

We talked fairly late and then went to our rooms. A fire burned in the grate of what I still thought of as my parents' bedroom and it seemed warm and welcoming. By then I'd guessed Ana had slept there for several nights. She slipped into the boudoir while I undressed in the bedroom, my head full of racing thoughts. I was in pyjamas and dressing-gown when Ana returned in nightie and negligée. She had removed her cosmetics and the scars and stitch-marks were very obtrusive on her pale skin.

Her blue eyes looked at me in a smile that seemed both shy and accepting as she came to me, still limping slightly, although they'd worked on her leg because she was barefoot, and her shoe needed to be built up a little. We clasped hands and I heard myself ask foolishly, 'Happy?'

She nodded, then said, 'But I'm sorry I'm not . . . more beautiful to be your wife.'

My heart was thumping and my voice husky when I answered, 'But you are beautiful,' and when I eased her negligée off her shoulders I knew that should have been true. The skin revealed by her sleeveless nightie was like white silk but it was marred by another of those damnable scars.

We kissed and touched each other sweetly and slowly for a little while and then moved to the bed. At one moment I was almost overawed by the knowledge I was making love to the daughter of an emperor.

For the next couple of days we became intensely aware of each other and I noticed Natasha giving us knowing little smiles. Then Mr Stott delivered the telegram which said, 'Unable contact you shipboard sorry interrupt your leave but desire urgent discussions arriving tomorrow afternoon regards Emery Porteous.'

I bit back some very nautical remarks. Now I had just discovered Ana the last thing I wanted was a snooping reporter. And what could he want? I thought momentarily of

Stefan's death but pushed it from my mind.

He arrived in a bull-nosed Morris coupé, then the latest in medium-income cars, and said proudly, 'The book's selling jolly well — now in third reprint — and so I've treated myself to this.'

He told me he had taken a room at The Swan, then the best of Fowlers Haven's three pubs and favoured by sporting shooters and fishermen. He said, 'I didn't realize you're such a big noise in these parts, and that you've brought a wife home from Russia.'

Silently I cursed whatever blabbermouth had been talking to him, and asked curtly, 'Why d'you want to see me?'

'Oh — sorry. My newspaper wants a series of articles on Russia to follow up on the book, and then they'll be reprinted as part of a new book. I thought if I could have a yarn with you, you might — '

'I'm afraid it's all confidential.'

'But I'm sure there must be some simple human interest. For example — when and where did you meet your wife and marry her in Bolshevik Russia? And I have the impression you know a lot more about Russia, past and present, than you've told me. I'd be grateful for your comments along those lines. Russia is such big news these days, you know.'

We were standing in front of the house, where I'd gone to meet him when I heard his car, and Natasha came out saying, 'Whatever are you doing out in the cold? Do come in by the fire.'

She led the way to the drawing-room, where Ana and Billy were already drinking tea in front of a roaring fire. Porteous, in good journalistic style, lost not a moment in ingratiating himself and asking questions which the others, naturally enough, answered readily. Someone had told him about the family's Russian connections and Natasha enjoyed boasting a little about our aristocratic connections in Russia. He was rather obviously steering the conversation towards my Russian experiences and he began by asking about family connections with the navy, my wartime experiences and so on. Ana, sitting next to me on a sofa, was a silent listener until he asked her suddenly, 'When did you first meet Benjamin?'

I was about to intervene but she answered calmly, 'Oh, I think it must have been about ten years ago.'

'Really? Where was that?'

'Both our families were holidaying on the Crimea.'

'And I suppose your own family were . . . ah . . . aristocrats?'

She smiled at that. 'Yes, you could say so.'

'I'd be awfully grateful for their ranks, and names, and so on just for reader interest, you know.'

Again I was about to intervene but she shook her head, saying, 'Sorry, better not.'

I felt her tense when he remarked, 'So many of the aristocracy have suffered so terribly. I've heard some appalling stories — especially about the Romanovs, of course.'

I'm sure he didn't know he was talking to one of them as he rambled on for a minute or so about 'the mystery of their disappearance'. No doubt he was only fishing but this subject led him on to the iniquities of the Cheka and then he asked me, 'Did you ever hear about a fellow named Iurovsky?'

Ana gave a little jerk at the name and he was a sufficiently skilled interviewer to sense the effect of his question on her. He looked back at her and was about to ask her something when Billy intervened with, 'Good God, is that the time? We're going out tonight, you know.'

That broke up the gathering and I escorted Porteous to the front door, where he said, 'I'd be awfully glad to talk to you a little more.'

I hesitated, then said, 'All right. I'll ring you at The Swan.'

When I returned to the drawing-room I

found Billy puffing at his pipe, and he growled, 'Appalling man. Journalists and politicians should be strangled at birth.' Of course we weren't going out and we spent a comfortable evening in, though Ana was more silent than usual. At bedtime she asked me, 'Will I have to talk to that man again?' I told her, 'Don't worry about it. I'll take care of him.'

She slept quietly by my side as I lay awake for a long time. I told myself that Porteous's mention of Iurovsky was, probably, only a side effect of the diet of gossip and rumour on which journalists flourish. No doubt someone had heard something about the Cheka man serving as jailer for the Romanovs and, after the execution of Nicholas, guessed at the rest of the story. Or perhaps one of the numerous drunks present at the disposal of the corpses had told his family, or a friend, all about it. Whatever the reason, I didn't like Porteous knowing about Iurovsky and felt he might have scented a story which could lead him . . . well, anywhere.

The north-east wind was rising when at last I fell asleep and when I awoke the icy wind was blowing under a high pale sky. My mind seemed to have been active while I was sleeping and it started to tell me what to do, presenting me with a plan which I'd trimmed and polished when I rang Porteous at The Swan and said, 'It's a great day for sailing — want to come along?'

He protested, 'I've never been sailing in my life, and it's bloody freezing!'

'Not as freezing as Moscow in winter. And I've remembered a few things you might like to hear about.'

Of course that was the bait which made him swallow the hook. I dressed in warm sailing gear, told Ana I'd be out for a couple of hours, and went down to the harbour. The family's boats had been laid up during the war, looked after by an old fisherman named Eric Cave, but I'd already asked him to launch and re-rig the twelve-foot dinghy. I was planning to introduce Ana to sailing.

The harbour of Fowlers Haven, once a busy little port, lay inside a tongue of land protruding halfway across the mouth of the River Fowler. When the tide was going out against the wind, adding its impetus to the river current, the combined forces whipped the entrance into sharp, angry little waves. When I picked up Porteous at The Swan I noticed that was just beginning to happen, ideal for my purpose.

Porteous wore a hairy tweed suit, tweed cap and overcoat and thick muffler, hardly suitable for sailing but perfect for my scheme.

Nowadays we would wear lifejackets but they were heavy clumsy items in the preplastics era and few people bothered with them.

Old Eric and I settled Porteous into the stern of the boat, Eric shoved us off and I hoisted the sails. The wind seemed to grab us and we shot away from the moorings, bouncing over the comparatively calm waters of the inner harbour. Porteous, like a good journalist, absorbed everything that was happening and, to my surprise, grinned at me and shouted, 'Hey, this is fun!'

I felt the pull of the tide strengthening as I sailed across the harbour and back, and warned Porteous to crouch down in the boat whenever I changed course and the boom of the sail swung over. I made two or three passes across the harbour, mainly to show old Eric I was giving Porteous some experience of sailing, until I decided conditions were right for what I intended to do.

Porteous stared intently ahead, his face reddened by the razor-sharp wind and wet with spray, at the turbulence where the wind slashed at the fast-moving outflow. The waves spurred up by the conflict of wind and water were sharp savage triangles capped with spray.

Just as we entered them he seemed to realize what could happen, or even what I intended to do to him. He turned and yelled at me but he was too late. The boat plunged into the maelstrom of waters and I simply let go of the tiller. The hull swung sideways, the boom whipped over and knocked Porteous overboard, and the wind in the sails capsized the little craft.

When I planned the operation I visualized myself clinging to the upturned boat. I'd be swept out to sea but hold on until Eric raised the alarm and I was rescued. But the tide was too strong and the waves too fierce and I was rushed seawards before I could grab any part of the boat or its rigging.

I tried to swim shorewards but the rushing current carried me out to sea. I just managed to keep my head above water that was close to freezing. Glimpses of the shore told me I was being driven further out, choking and gasping in the tumultuous waters.

I struggled to swim across the confused wave pattern into calmer waters but the cold defeated me. It seemed to deaden my heart and lungs and paralyse my will. At last I was conscious that the force of the tide race was slackening in the open sea but I was almost too exhausted to take advantage of this. I could only just hear the shouts from a passing trawler, homeward bound for Great Yarmouth with a load of herrings, when a couple of crewmen spotted my head amongst the waves.

20

Local lifesavers tried to find Porteous's body but without success. The tide race must have swept him out into deep water. I felt no remorse because I thought that, intentionally or otherwise, he was a possible troublemaker, likely to ferret out Ana's background for use in his book.

Natasha was the only person to show any suspicion. On the day after the 'accident' she said abruptly to me, 'Ana told that man Porteous she first met you in the Crimea, when she was a little girl.'

I guessed what was coming and said, 'She had to tell him something.'

'Yes, but ... the only children I can remember meeting there were those of the royal family.'

'Oh, come off it! We had umpteen relations staying with us, plus children's parties and so on.'

'Yes, but I specially remember meeting the royal children. The youngest of them would be about Ana's age now. Her name was Anastasia, too.'

'It's a common enough Russian name.'

'I know, but ... well, she's so very unwilling to talk about herself. I can't help thinking there's something ... well, almost mysterious about her.'

With feigned anger I said, 'All you need to know is that Ana had a terrible time in Russia, that Stefan and I met her when we were there on a confidential mission, and if I say too much I might betray that confidence. So could you please stop making up stories like some gossiping old woman?'

I went in search of Ana and told her about Natasha's comments. She looked downcast, saying, 'I'm sorry. I should never have made up that silly story about how I met you.'

'Well, never mind that. It's what you said about meeting me years ago that made her suspicious.'

She sighed. 'I knew I was making a mistake when I heard myself saying those things. It was just that — well, when he asked the question I found myself wanting to tell the truth.'

'Then don't you think it may be time for us to tell the true story? It's almost certain to come out somehow.'

The fear on her face made me sorry I'd spoken.

'No — please! You know how terrible the Reds can be — they'd come for me if they knew where I am!'

I tried to reason with her but it only distressed her. She was convinced that, since she was the sole direct heir to the Russian throne, the Reds would want to destroy her.

I apologized to Natasha, saying, 'I'm sorry I was rude but it's a tricky situation. Still very confidential.'

In a challenging elder sister tone she asked, 'So confidential that Stefan had to be shot, and Mr Porteous drowned?'

I managed to fake a laugh. 'Don't be ridiculous!'

'Then tell me who paid for months of hospital treatment for Ana? You couldn't have done it on a lieutenant's pay and you haven't drawn much out of the estate accounts.'

I was reduced to mumbling, 'I can't see it's any of your business.'

She said calmly, 'Perhaps not. But you're the male heir to the Knyve estate, and you and Ana may have babies, and the rest of the family have the right to know what's happening.'

She paused, then said, 'I'm sure you know a good many of the Russian aristocracy have managed to escape — unfortunately not including any of our relations.'

I nodded. There had been plenty of newspaper stories, and I had heard that Ana's grandmother, the dowager empress, was now living in Denmark together with some other relations.

Natasha continued, 'Then why hasn't Ana tried to find any of her relations amongst those who've escaped? Or why haven't they tried to find her? Do they know she's married to an Englishman? And would they recognize her after that plastic surgery?'

I was horrified to realize this confrontation was actually making me feel I should dispose of Natasha as I had disposed of Stefan and Porteous. I lit a cigarette, and smoked for a few moments before I said, 'Well, I can only tell you what I did before. It's confidential. I promise to tell you about it when I can.'

She said drily, 'I think I can guess it anyway.'

'Then you'll know it's important to keep it quiet.'

At bedtime I told Ana, 'I think it would be a good idea if you came back to Chatham with me when I rejoin the *Spartan*. We'll find a nice place for you to live ashore and you'll soon make friends with the other officers' wives.'

She nodded, murmuring, 'All right . . . if you think it's best.'

'And . . . I wish you'd think about us telling the true story. Think of your grandmother and other relations. They'd be so happy to hear you're alive.'

She protested, 'No, no! I've thought about it so much. It would be terrible. The Whites who've escaped from Russia would want me to be their leader in exile, and that would make the Reds even more determined to do away with me.'

I tried to laugh that off, saying there'd be plenty of people to look after her on a naval base, but she'd go no further than, 'Maybe in a year or two. I'm so happy in the life you've made for us — don't make me change it yet.'

I had to request an extension of leave in order to attend the inquest on the death of Porteous, which was readily granted because there was little occupation for ships of the Home Fleet. I told the Coroner, 'Mr Porteous seemed to be enjoying himself and so I sailed into the tide race, to let it carry us out to sea. We could have sailed out there until the tide race slackened and the wind carried us back into harbour. Unfortunately Mr Porteous . . . well, lost his head in the rough water. He grabbed for the tiller and I lost control of the boat, and it capsized.'

Local opinion was that I'd been unlucky rather than reckless. The inquest verdict was of death by misadventure and it didn't even reprimand me. Luckily Porteous was unmarried and survived only by a couple of relations, who seemed rather pleased by the prospect of inheriting his book royalties and his new car.

I returned to HMS *Spartan*, planning to arrange for Ana to live in or near Chatham. But I'd only been back on duty for a few days when I was astonished by orders to leave the *Spartan* and take command of HMS *Gnat*, a river gunboat in China.

I suspected Blaze and his mentors might have arranged this forward step in my navy career though I had to leave Ana behind. Wartime losses in passenger ships had not yet been replaced and there were long waiting lists for travel by sea.

I was able to snatch a few more days at home before leaving England. Apparently Natasha had decided to bury her suspicions and she was quite amiable, while Ana put on a brave face when I explained she could follow me as soon as possible. She wept a little on my last night and my efforts to console her merged into very sweet and tender lovemaking. Somehow 'taking precautions' would have seemed inappropriate and I was unwilling to interrupt the exquisite progress towards consummation.

21

Next day I travelled to Tilbury and boarded a P&O liner, which was crammed with passengers bound for various parts of the British Empire. The six-week voyage to Shanghai was long and tedious, though interrupted by calls at the chain of empire ports from Gibraltar to Hong Kong.

One morning the ship's bows breasted the flood of yellow water at the mouth of the mighty Yangtze River, ending its 3000-mile run from Tibet. The liner went upriver to the mouth of the tributary Whangpoo, where passengers for Shanghai boarded a steam tender. We soon experienced the characteristic reek of China from the 'foo-foo barges' of human manure being towed down river for use on gardens and farms.

Shanghai was a huge city even then, a by-product of foreign exploitation mainly by Britain, America, France and Japan. The 'foreign devils', greedy for trade, had destroyed the ancient empire, and by the 1920s China was ruled by warlords and a fragmented government partly controlled by foreigners. The British, for example, ran the

Customs Department efficiently and profitably.

Shanghai was home base for a number of gunboats, and some other military forces, operating under the flags of the foreign countries principally interested in protecting their trade along the Yangtze. They also safeguarded the foreign 'concessions', consulates, hospitals and missionary stations established at a number of places along the great river.

When I landed from the passenger tender I was pleased to find a petty officer from the *Gnat* awaiting me. He'd reserved a taxi to carry me and my baggage and as I boarded it I noticed a trio of Europeans, apparently waterside clerks, standing nearby and talking in Russian. I asked the PO, 'Are there many Russians in China?', and he replied, 'Thousands of the poor buggers, sir. Swarming across the borders to get away from the Reds, and taking any jobs they can find.'

The taxi took us through teeming streets and delivered us to the *Gnat*, then secured alongside and taking on provisions and deck and engineroom supplies. I'd never seen anything like this warship and for a couple of minutes I surveyed her from the dockside. The river gunboats, which some comedian in the Admiralty had christened *Ant, Fly, Bee,*

Gnat and so on, had been designed especially for service on the Yangtze. The square-sterned hull, shaped like a flat iron, drew only four feet of water. Three large rectangular rudders, operating simultaneously, gave instant manoeuvrability. The twin screws were housed in tunnels, to protect them from rocky bottoms or floating debris. The armament of two four-inch guns apiece, plus weapons for landing parties, made the gunboats a real threat to bandits, rebel armies, revolutionaries, and other disturbers of the peace.

Jim Lucas, the commander of the *Gnat* whom I was relieving, welcomed me vociferously. He said, 'We're under orders to proceed upstream tomorrow morning, and if you hadn't turned up on time I'd've been in for another trip up the Yangtze!'

I changed into white tropical uniform while he assembled the ship's company to hear me 'read myself in'. The *Gnat*'s total complement of one lieutenant junior in seniority to me, a sub-lieutenant, two petty officers for engineering duties and two for the deck, and eighteen ratings with various qualifications, listened solemnly as I read out my Admiralty orders to assume command of the gunboat.

A celebratory dinner for the officers, served on deck because it was too hot to eat down below, was provided by two white-jacketed

Chinese stewards. I'd already noticed a number of Chinese working around the ship and I asked Lucas, 'Are these Chinese part of the ship's company?'

'No, they simply sail with us and do all the dirty work. Washing, cooking, cleaning, painting, down the engine-room and so on.'

'But who pays them?'

'All of us. All the officers and men chip in a few dollars per month apiece. There's usually enough food for them to have a share and they sleep wherever they can find a nook or cranny. Makes life easier for us and gives them some kind of a living.'

'Hmm . . . doesn't sound too good for discipline, though.'

Lucas laughed. 'You'd be surprised. The old navy hands have never been so comfortable and they wouldn't risk a transfer by slacking off.'

I had already noticed the *Gnat* was immaculate with glistening paint and brass-work, snowy deck planks and canvas awnings.

Lucas left next morning and I inherited his steward, a handsome young Chinese with some command of English whose name was Wing Wang.

Lieutenant 'Titus' Oates, my second-in-command, tended to hover over me when we left our berth and turned into the main-stream, which was as busy as Piccadilly

Circus with countless Chinese junks and sampans, strings of foo-foo barges full or empty, ocean tramps and oil tankers, ferry boats and river passenger steamers. But everything went smoothly until an approaching Chinese junk abruptly altered course and crossed our bows, its crew yelling derisively while ours shouted insults. I exclaimed, 'What the bloody hell — '

Titus explained, 'They do that to get rid of the devils that hang on to a ship's stern. After a while there's a whole string of devils streaming along behind, holding on to each other hand in hand and causing all kinds of bad luck. But they reckon our bows will have cut off the devils and taken their bad luck aboard.'

We steamed out into the mighty Yangtze and turned upriver, heading for the small port of Tsan Tsi where we were to spend the night. When we arrived at our anchorage we found two sampans full of young Chinese men and women getting in our way and Titus said, 'Bloody Kuomintang students. Shall we rig hoses to get rid of them?'

I said, 'Whatever's customary,' and watched the students unroll cotton banners on which Chinese characters were painted. I asked him, 'What's Kuomintang?'.

'Nationalist Party. They want us out of China.'

Wing Wang had just brought me a cup of tea and I asked him, 'What do those characters mean that are written on the banners?'

He giggled, then said, 'Those in one boat say *Kui men ai dao*. Means . . . hmm .. 'We opened door and thieves came in.''

'And the other?'

I didn't know a Chinese could blush but he flushed pink under his ivory skin. Giggling again, he said, 'It say: 'Foreign — ah — bad word — go back own country.''

'What's the bad word?'

He tittered 'Holes in beneath part.'

Titus translated, ''Foreign arseholes go home.' I'll get the hoses turned on the local variety.'

22

There was no airmail to China in those days and Ana's letters could take a couple of months to reach me in one of the river ports. She was more than three months pregnant by the time I heard the news, including her doctor's advice against the sea voyage to Shanghai.

Of course I was disappointed but I had many other things to think about. I was determined to succeed in my first command and 'learning the river' kept me on my toes. The Yangtze winds through many types of country and its depths and currents, ranging from waist-deep to disastrous flooding, depend on the weather and the seasons of the year. At that time no one had drawn reliable charts of the river and one had to learn its vagaries by experience and observation.

Thousands of foreigners then lived along the Yangtze, mostly in the 'concessions' which were European-type communities established in the principal ports. I never saw the legendary sign 'Dogs and Chinese prohibited' but that was certainly the attitude of the concessions. Sikh police, officered by Britons, kept out any Chinese apart from domestic servants and other employees.

Gunboat officers, who symbolized protection for communities surrounded by Chinese, were welcome in the European clubs and as partners in dances, bridge parties, and cricket and tennis matches.

Chinese government, at a time when the Kuomintang confronted the communists and both parties wanted to expel foreigners, was chaotic. The warlords with their private armies squeezed bribes out of Chinese businessmen while the provincial governments sometimes weren't much better than the gangs of bandits and river pirates.

My first encounter with the latter came on a sticky sultry morning when the *Gnat* made her way up a broad stretch of river, with green rice paddies stretching away on both sides. A lookout reported, 'That there sampan's giving us a hail!', and my binoculars showed me a white man signalling wildly from the little craft. When we came closer Titus said, 'That's Roger Camden from Forty-Four Rocks,' which was the name of a reef projecting into the river and also for a nearby American nonconformist mission.

When Camden scrambled aboard he proclaimed, 'Praise the Lord! I was praying for help and here you are — an answer to a prayer!'

I hardly thought the Lord had planted the *Gnat* there as proof of his existence but Camden was in a highly excitable condition, and his white shirt and trousers were splotched with blood from a flesh wound. He gabbled, 'They're pirates — Chi'en Cheng's men. They turned up about an hour ago, just after a couple of American journalists turned up at the mission. Hey, look — there's their boat!'

A large motor boat, with a cabin forward and the stars and stripes on its jackstaff, drifted slowly round the bend. Camden said, 'There were two white men and two Chinese — one of the Chinese cut the boat adrift but the pirates shot him, and the boat drifted away.'

We took the boat alongside and saw a corpse in its cockpit, then took it in tow. Camden rattled on, 'Chi'en Cheng told Reverend Smithfield, who's our principal, he'd burn down the mission if we didn't hand over all our food and money and ten of our girls.' He meant the girls whom peasants sold or gave to the missions as babies, to be brought up and educated and eventually married to Chinese Christians. Otherwise their parents would have abandoned them to die as 'useless mouths'.

Camden said, 'Anyway, I slipped away when they were arguing. One of them fired at me but I only got this flesh wound.'

Another bend in the river brought us to the mission, which lay behind a clump of trees on the river bank. Smoke rose above the trees and Camden wailed, 'They've set fire to the mission!'

I'd given all the necessary orders by the time we headed for the mission landing stage. The pirate junk was tied up alongside and those aboard were foolish enough to fire an erratic volley. I ordered one round from each of our guns and the result was spectacular. Deck planks and bodies flew in all directions, the junk burst into flames and drifted downstream, and Camden shouted joyously, 'That'll teach you to affront the Lord!'

Wing Wang brought me my revolver-belt and as I buckled it on I told Titus, 'Put us alongside — I'll lead the landing party. You follow with a fire party as soon as you've made fast.'

The mission consisted of several buildings and a church built around a courtyard. The main building faced the river across a strip of garden. When I jumped ashore and towards it, revolver in hand, a big Chinese clad only in cotton trousers appeared in the doorway. He levelled a rifle at me but I fired first, with a strange thrill of pleasure when the bullet hole appeared in his bare chest and he tumbled backwards. We trampled over him as we ran into the house and through the passage leading into the courtyard.

Smithfield, nursing a bleeding head, sat on the ground in front of a group of Chinese and Americans. To my astonishment I saw that Grigor Peskov was amongst them. A group of pirates was guarding them and several more pirates were trying to herd a large bunch of teenage Chinese girls, who were crying and wailing and even throwing themselves down, out of the courtyard.

The pirates guarding Smithfield and his staff threw down their weapons and held up their hands as soon as we appeared, while the ones kidnapping the teenage girls immediately ran away. But a shot was fired from an open ground-floor window, without hitting anyone, and Smithfield said, 'That's Chi'en and a couple of his gang, trying to open the safe in my office.'

I told my men, 'Let 'em have it — make them keep their heads down,' and they responded with gusto. One carried a bag of Mills bombs and I told him, 'Try to put one through the window.' He flung the bomb with the action of an overarm bowler and it flew in through the window, exploded, and sent a gush of burning paper and furniture fragments out into the courtyard plus several body parts including a hand.

Titus and several others suddenly burst into the courtyard, dragging a hose with them. They had linked several lengths of our three-inch canvas hoses together and the result was just long enough to send a jet of water, pumped from the *Gnat*, arching out of the brass nozzle. The mission men helped our fire crew to save the church from destruction.

Smithfield, rising shakily to his feet, said solemnly, 'God bless you.' Grigor, grinning broadly, pushed forward and held out his hand. I took it and shook it and asked, 'What the dev — I mean what on earth are you doing here?'

'We call ourselves journalists, because that's something everyone understands. Meet my partner, Arthur Pierrot.'

Pierrot was a young, handsome man, who smiled gratefully at me as he shook my hand. He said, 'We do work for a group of American newspapers, on what you might call a roving commission, and all this will be a mighty good story for them. But we're mainly representing a New York organization that's trying to help Russian refugees in China. That's what we're doing along the river, trying to find out how many are in concessions and missions and so on.'

Smithfield insisted on us staying overnight and on treating us to a modest feast, plus choral entertainment by the girls who, as Smithfield said, we had saved from 'a fate worse than death'.

Pierrot told me something about the Russian refugees. Some, such as business reps and consular staff, had been in China since before the war but had now been abandoned by their homeland. Many others were those who had fled Bolshevism in the hope of settling in China, only to find there was no work for them in the chaotic over-populated country. Pierrot said, 'Our organization hopes that Britain, France and the USA, and maybe some other countries, will put together some kind of rescue scheme when we have all the data.'

Next morning we saw him and Grigor, and the surviving crewman, off in the hired motor boat they were returning to a concession. Our run to the nearest port included the unpleasant task of delivering those pirates we'd taken prisoner to what was likely to be very swift justice, by the executioner's sword.

Grigor and Pierrot sent the story to their newspapers and we began to receive letters and small gifts from supporters of the mission.

The hot summer mellowed into autumn, the green rice fields turned gold and were full of harvesters, and river levels fell as distant tributaries froze. I was becoming impatient for news of the baby, which was expected in early November. Mail deliveries were so slow I'd arranged for Natasha to send me a cablegram with the news, and it was eventually relayed through the telegraph office at Hankow. It said: 'So sorry darling. Baby stillborn Ana recovering well love Natasha.'

There's nothing to do about such disappointments except accept them, and the routine of duty helped me do that. Winter was icy cold and we wore heavy clothing, while coal stoves kept our accommodation warm. Great flocks of ducks, pheasant and other birds came down river and provided recreational shooting and much-needed variety to the *Gnat's* menus.

Ana's letters revived the prospect of her joining me in China but I was uncertain. I thought one of the refugees might somehow recognize her and, deliberately or otherwise, betray her. In such an event the Reds might target her to prevent her from becoming a rallying point for the Whites, or simply as heir to the throne. The growth of communism in China seemed to increase the danger.

I didn't mention such worries in my letters to Ana but simply remarked on the refugees and thought she'd work the rest out for herself. I also told her about problems in finding accommodation and my long absences on river patrols. But she persisted, and when she wrote to say she had managed to book a liner passage I was spurred into action. I found a flat in the concession at Ichang, belonging to a French couple who would be returning home on long leave at about the time Ana was expected to arrive. I also contrived for the *Gnat* to be in Shanghai at that time. The ship would be due for annual overhaul and maintenance work, known as 'refitting', in the dry dock used by the navy at Shanghai.

We berthed there on the day before Ana was due to arrive and I reported to the naval agent, Commander Purvis. A cheerful and cooperative individual, he welcomed me by handing me a printed list of names and saying, 'This'll make you happy.' It was a notification of recent promotions, including mine to lieutenant-commander. Purvis said, 'You'll probably receive the official bumf in the next mail,' and insisted on celebrating my promotion by inviting me and Ana to dinner on the following evening.

Next day I stood on the waterfront as the passenger tender disgorged its usual throng of new arrivals, ranging from 'Old China Hands' looking bored and sophisticated to youngsters arriving for the first time. I couldn't see Ana until a prettily-dressed young woman asked me, 'Hallo, Ben — don't you recognize me?'

In fact I would hardly have recognized her. High-heeled shoes, which she would previously have found uncomfortable because of her limp, made her look taller. Her long brown hair had been 'bobbed', as they said in the 1920s. Her hat and clothes were more fashionable than anything I'd seen her wearing before. Her scars and stitches had begun to fade but were still visible, and probably always would be because plastic surgery was cruder then than now, but she had used cosmetics to disguise them.

Her blue eyes were large and amused, her body seemed fuller and more mature and yet more poised and graceful. She seemed very different from the shrinking disfigured teenager I still remembered.

I stammered something and she offered her lips for my kiss. They moved under mine and I felt an instant sexual reaction, and jerked away with an embarrassed little laugh.

I'd booked us in at the Carlton Hotel, then one of the newest and flashiest of the city's many hotels. We had some lunch there but neither of us seemed to want very much and we talked rather disjointedly until we went up to our room. There, in its privacy, all the things we knew and felt about each other were able to flow freely between us.

Eventually we went to our dinner with Commander and Martina Purvis. They took us to the Shanghai Club, a big palatial building favoured by the more prosperous members of Shanghai's non-Chinese community. Martina was a rather dominating personality but Ana seemed to know instinctively how to comport herself towards the wife of an officer senior to her husband, and Martina thawed quickly and poured out advice for a young lady about to reside in China.

Our stay in Shanghai could not be long, because the Chinese drydock contractors worked round the clock on the *Gnat*. But it was the first opportunity Ana and I had had to spend time undisturbedly together and we seemed able to talk more freely than before. I mentioned my fear of a refugee recognizing her but she said, 'I don't think there's much chance of that now. It's five years since the Reds prevented me and my family from being seen by the rest of the people, at first near Moscow and then in Siberia. I've changed very much since then and not only from my . . . injuries.'

I said, 'Yes, you've become even more beautiful,' which led to a fairly long break in the conversation. Later I asked whether she wanted to see her grandmother and other surviving relations and she thought for a while before saying, 'Not yet, anyway. What if the newspapers found out? It might put all of us in danger.'

The newspapers, in fact, cast a shadow over our last day together in Shanghai. One of the English-speaking dailies carried a report that the Berlin police had saved an attempted suicide from drowning in a canal, and taken her to hospital. At first she would not reveal her name but then she began hinting she was Anastasia Romanov, youngest daughter of the Emperor Nicholas.

When Ana read the story she went so pale that her scars stood out vividly. I embraced her, trying to console her, and felt her trembling. She asked, 'Why should anyone pretend to be me? Do they want to be as sad, and lost, as I feel sometimes?'

I kissed her gently, saying, 'Don't worry about it. If someone in Germany says she's you, then people in China are less likely to suspect you're the real Anastasia.'

She said fiercely, 'Then I hope the Reds kill her instead of me!', and burst into tears.

23

Next morning I took her to the passenger steamer which carried her up to Ichang. Mrs Treloar, wife of the British consul in Ichang, had kindly offered to meet her and help her settle in.

Our rendezvous was delayed longer than I'd expected. The Nationalists began fighting the warlord who controlled the Nanking area and we had to stand by in case the conflict overflowed into the concession. When the Nationalists had overwhelmed the warlord they turned their attention to us, and obstructed our progress upriver with swarms of junks and sampans. Their crews beat gongs and drums, blew trumpets, yelled slogans, and flew banners with phrases that, so Wing Wang told me, were all variations on the phrase, 'White persons quickly leave China!'

I worried as to how Ana was getting on but when at last we reached Ichang I found her in good spirits. The people of the small concession were pleased to welcome a new face and she was becoming interested in Chinese art. She and one of her new friends often went horseriding and a Chinese tailor had made her a pair of the riding breeches known as jodhpurs. They were a novelty for women then, and rather deplored by the older generation, but they certainly suited her shapely thighs and bottom.

Ichang was far up the river and comparatively isolated, and out of the usual routes of Russian refugees. This eased our worries on that score but, as I soon discovered, she was emphatic that we must not yet have another baby. She said, 'The hospital here is small and not very well equipped, so we'd be taking a risk if anything went wrong. And . . . well, if I did need to leave in a hurry, it would be better if I wasn't pregnant or with a baby in arms.'

We soon adjusted to a lifestyle in which my river patrols brought me home to her at irregular intervals. Most of the ship's company had similar arrangements, though they were mostly with Chinese, Eurasian or even Russian sleeping partners at various ports along the river.

So the months passed, through another long sweaty summer into cool golden autumn and frigid winter. The separations, often for weeks at a time, gave special zest to those moments when Ana and I could snuggle up in the French couple's double bed.

The *Gnat* often spent a couple of hours

alongside the Forty-Four Rocks mission landing stage, where Mr and Mrs Smithfield liked to welcome us. They often gave us bundles of American magazines, with titles long defunct since the advent of TV, and on one of these my eye caught the cover wording, 'Is Anastasia Alive? See Page 42.'

Of course I devoured the article, which said that the girl who claimed to be Anastasia had now expanded on her story. She said she had been rescued from the Cheka by a Russian soldier who had taken her to Bucharest, where she lived with him until she ran away and reached Berlin. She was trying to contact 'relations' who now lived in western Europe, but those surviving members of the imperial family, and others who had known the real Anastasia, could never agree on her identity. Some swore she was the emperor's youngest daughter while others scoffed at the idea.

The story, one of the first of countless books and articles to be written about the claimant, took a neutral stance but made an interesting suggestion: that she might have a claim to the fortune in gold roubles which Nicholas had deposited in the Bank of England. As we steamed away upriver I couldn't stop the story running through my head. Was it possible the claimant was the real Anastasia, and that Ana was . . . well, perhaps a servant girl included in the massacre by the Cheka? But my Anastasia spoke perfect English, in a manner likely to have been taught to royal children but not to servants, and there was something in her blue eyes which made me think she was the little girl I'd met on the beach at Livadia.

I couldn't decide whether to show the story to Ana or not, but by the time we reached Ichang again I'd decided it was nonsense and I wouldn't worry her with it. And we had other things to think about. The French couple who had let their flat to us would soon be returning to Ichang, while my two-year appointment in the *Gnat* was nearing its end. The time came when I was advised that my replacement was leaving England.

Ana began to pack up the possessions we'd accumulated and I looked up the passenger-ship sailings to London. But before I made a booking, Commander Purvis relayed to me an offer in which I detected the fine hand of Captain — now Rear-Admiral — Blaze. It was for my appointment as RN Liaison Officer to the Royal Australian Navy, with headquarters in Sydney.

When I discussed it with Ana I told her, 'I've got a notion your English royal relations still feel concerned about you. The Whites have been defeated in Russia but they're still trying to arouse support against the Reds, and you might — well, become some kind of pawn in the game. The royals might have asked Blaze to arrange something that will keep you out of harm's way.'

She said doubtfully, 'Yes, but . . . Australia? I don't know anything about the place and I can't think what it would be like to live there.'

I'd met Australians during the war, at Gallipoli and elsewhere, and liked and respected them. But the angle I used with Ana was that the appointment would be a step forward in my career and might lead to better things.

She agreed somewhat reluctantly, and after that the time passed quickly until the morning when we stood on the upper deck of the *Loh Ning*, one of the many British-owned cargo-passenger ships trading on the China coast from the Gulf of Korea to the Gulf of Tonkin. She was not a large ship, carrying only twenty-four passengers in the first-class cabins, but she was modern and comfortable.

The *Loh Ning* was taking Ana and me to Hong Kong to board a ship from Sydney. Mr Bedell, the ship's second officer, stood beside us talking about pirates. We were looking down on the ship's after deck, where a swarm of Chinese passengers sought relief from their overcrowded quarters. Bedell said, 'Look at 'em! You can't tell whether they're families and labour gangs heading for their home villages after a few years in Shanghai, or whether some of them are a bunch of pirates waiting to take over the ship.'

Like most Europeans in China in those days I'd heard about the system in which a gang of pirates boarded a ship as steerage-class passengers, and took her over if opportunity served. But I pointed to the high metal grille, topped with barbed wire and fitted with a couple of locked gates, which separated the steerage area from the rest of the ship, and said, 'Well, you seem to be well protected.'

'Oh, sure. And we have half a dozen armed Sikh policemen aboard to keep watch on the steerage, and all the officers are armed. But I tell you what, if old John Chinaman wants something he'll go after it, come what may, and he can be a nasty bugger if he doesn't get it.'

He told us that pirates set fire to ships whose crews resisted too vigorously. If they managed to take over they took the ship into one of the pirate villages along the coast, such as Bias Bay or Chilang, looted her and let her sail away again.

Ana asked, 'But why do the ships take on Chinese workmen as passengers if they might be pirates?', and Bedell replied, 'Only a small percentage of ships are pirated and I suppose the ship owners reckon the profits are worth the risk, and the insurance companies can take up the slack.'

He went off about his duties and Ana and I linked arms and strolled up and down the snowy planking of the upper deck. I was happy with the prospect of Australia, as a civilized country far separated from the antagonisms of the northern hemisphere, while Ana was happy because she now understood that the post of liaison officer would be a 'shore job' in which I'd spend little time at sea. She'd asked, 'Will we be able to have a house and live together properly?', and smiled contentedly when I replied, 'I expect so, but I don't know anything about the cost of housing and so on.'

'Don't forget about those jewels of mine, now safe in the bank at home. I expect we could sell some if necessary.'

I said, 'Oh, I doubt whether it'll come to that,' because I felt that offering the jewels for sale might arouse awkward questions. I still had no idea why I'd been offered the Australian appointment, which was a plum job in its way, instead of the usual routine of a spell of home leave followed by a shore job or seagoing position. Whatever the reason, I was glad of it, and looked forward to seeing more of the world.

Next morning the ship berthed in Amoy, now known as Xiamen, which was the last of our ports of call *en route* to Hong Kong. We were to sail again that evening and the cargo winches clattered busily at discharging and loading freight. I noticed that one of the railway trucks ranged along the wharf was loaded with small solidly made boxes and that it had an armed guard. I asked Bedell, 'What are those?', and he answered, 'Chests of opium. Going to Europe to make into morphia and such. Worth a bloody fortune.'

When sailing time drew near I stood on the upper deck with Ana, watching preparations for departure including the arrival of some new passengers. One of them, walking across the gangway, glanced up as though sensing he was being watched. He was Grigor Peskov, followed by Arthur Pierrot. They recognized me and waved and smiled a greeting.

When I told Ana about the episode at Forty-Four Rocks I hadn't mentioned Grigor. Somehow I felt he was best forgotten. I'd simply described him and Arthur as 'Two Americans', and outlined their reasons for being in China. Now, when she asked me, 'Who are those two men?', I told her, 'The two Yanks I told you about, who were at Forty-Four Rocks.'

I almost added 'Don't you remember Grigor?' but still thought it best to say nothing. We rarely talked about our escape from Russia, of which Ana seemed only to have dim memories. The only incident she ever questioned me about, several times and at some length, was our marriage in the Perm cathedral.

Grigor, with a ruddy smiling face and a smartly tailored suit, looked very different from the unshaven refugee with a black eye and dilapidated garments. Just as Ana looked very different from the wretched teenager crouched in the bows of the boat, trying to prevent anyone from seeing her injured face. I wondered whether they would recognize each other, and what they would make of each other in this very different time and place.

24

Grigor, as I later thought of it, made the first move. A steward brought a note to our cabin saying, 'For old times' sake we would be delighted if you and Mrs Knyve would join us in the smoke-room for a drink before dinner — Grigor.'

I showed it to Ana and she asked, 'Who's Grigor?'

'Probably you don't remember him. He helped us get the boat to escape down the river from Kotlas.'

'Oh. All right, then.'

She showed little interest until we entered the smoke-room and the two men rose to greet us. When I introduced them, Grigor held her hand unnecessarily long and stared intently at her, chattering such wording as, 'My word, you look very different from the first time I saw you or didn't really see you, ha ha! — and I can see Benjamin's taking really good care of you!'

Apparently he had already described the escape to Arthur but he persisted in talking about it, at annoying length, while we consumed a couple of pre-dinner drinks. For much of the time Ana sat silent, eyes downcast, except when Grigor said, incredibly, to me, 'I can see now why poor Ana had to keep her poor face covered up in those days!'

She flushed angrily, causing the marks on her face to stand out beneath her make-up. I was about to say something but a steward entered the smoke-room sounding the dinner-gong, and I was able to start standing up. But Grigor exclaimed, 'There's a couple of seats vacant at our table and I asked the chief steward to shift you over for dinner — after all, we'll be in Hong Kong tomorrow and I didn't want to miss this chance to chat about old times!'

Without outright rudeness there seemed no way to refuse, and I thought we could simply get the evening over quickly. To my surprise, Grigor seemed to check his babbling when we sat down to dinner, though I could see his thoughtful stares at Ana were annoying her. Arthur kept the conversation going, talking about their experiences in trying to raise money for the refugees. They hoped the Hong Kong businessmen would be generous.

As dinner ended the passengers began to drift away to the smokeroom, where coffee was served, but Ana said, 'I'm so sleepy, Ben — I'm going straight to our cabin,' and

Arthur chimed in with, 'It's been a long day for me too.' I might have followed them but Grigor said quickly, 'Just spare a minute, Ben. There's something I want to say to you.'

He insisted on ordering brandy to go with our coffee, but seemed in no hurry to talk as we sat and smoked and drank. He rambled on with pointless conversation, ordered more brandy, and eventually took a piece of newsprint from an inside pocket. It was a page from the small-format American magazine *Liberty*, now long defunct, and I saw it was yet another article about the young woman claiming to be Anastasia. But this one included a photograph of the impostor, which had very little resemblance to the real thing.

I skimmed through the article, noticing that the final paragraph mentioned the Romanov fortune allegedly deposited in Britain and speculated on whether Anastasia would claim it, and handed it back to Grigor. I put a bored inflection in my voice as I asked, 'What about it?'

'Well, I can tell you this photo doesn't look a bit like the real Anastasia.'

'How do you know?'

'Because I've seen her, that's why. When she was about sixteen. I was running the business then but it was hard to get stock after the revolution started, though things weren't as bad as they got later on. I travelled around seeing what I could pick up and I was on the Tobolsk railway station when the Reds sent the Romanovs there. I had a good look at all of them and I saw Anastasia was a pretty young girl, with blue eyes and long blonde hair and thick eyebrows, almost meeting across her forehead.'

He swigged at his drink. 'When we were in the boat together I saw the top part of your wife's face now and again, when she let the veil slip down. And she had blue eyes and thick eyebrows just like Anastasia's.'

'What are you getting at?'

'Well, I reckon your wife looks a lot more like Anastasia than the girl in that photograph does. And when I saw her this afternoon, when she was standing next to you and looking down at the passengers crossing the gangway, I thought she had a real look of Anastasia about her. That's why I got that magazine article out of my file, to show it to you.'

By that time the smoke-room was empty apart from a sleepy steward and a couple of tables of bridge players, totally intent on their game. Grigor glanced around at them and then shifted his chair closer to mine, leaning across to me and saying confidentially, 'Don't you understand? I could say I was in the boat with you after you'd rescued Anastasia, and I recognized her because I'd seen her in Tobolsk and helped you to get her to safety, and so on.'

'But why should we make up a yarn like that?'

'God, you're slow, aren't you? So she can claim all that money in the Bank of England! I'd be your witness, and help to coach Ana in the story and make it believable. I'd say we have a better chance of putting it across than that other girl. I could organize everything for . . . well, a small percentage.'

I said, 'I'll bet you could,' and I was standing up just when we heard the shot. It was muted, because it was up on the bridge deck, and I heard later it was the shot which killed the ship's wireless operator. Then there was a fusillade of shots, loud and shocking, and everyone was running out of the smoke-room down to their cabins. I found Ana sitting up in her bunk with her blue eyes wide, and she demanded, 'What's happening? Have you been all this time with that horrible man Grigor?'

I said, 'The ship's being pirated. Quick — get up and dress.'

I took my service revolver and ammunition from my briefcase and slipped cartridges into the cylinder. Ana slipped off her nightie and began to pull on her clothes, and even in that moment I was conscious of the scars on her white body. The thought flashed through my mind: Grigor would love to see them to support his story.

Other passengers were moving confusedly around in the alleyway outside the cabins. One, a man named Eggars who was a planter from Malaya (as we always called it in those days), also held a pistol. Asian officials rarely questioned your possession of such weapons so long as you were a respectable white man. But when Grigor and Arthur pushed down the alleyway, and I saw the Luger automatic in Grigor's hand, I thought the number of weapons in a confined space was becoming dangerous. I was about to say so when we heard another outburst of firing.

In the *Loh Ning* the crew lived in the fo'c'sle and were mostly off duty at that time. Unarmed, they wisely kept their heads down. The Chinese passengers, about a hundred, lived in the stern. We first-class passengers were housed amidships, in the three-tier structure above the engine room. It also contained the captain's and officers' quarters, the doctor's surgery and ship's office, and was topped by the boat-deck, navigation bridge and wireless room.

This was the area fenced off from the

Chinese passengers and supposedly guarded by the Sikh policemen. I heard later they'd been ambushed when changing watch.

I was hoping the renewed firing meant the ship's officers were fighting back when I heard Bedell's voice gasping 'Let me through!' and he came shoving along the alleyway, clad only in pyjamas and seaboots and bleeding from a cut in the head. He panted, 'We gotta do something. Bastards've killed the skipper and young Sparks. Third Officer's trapped in the wheelhouse and the others've been locked in their rooms.'

He fingered the cut in his head. 'I copped this when I was getting away and it made me drop my pistol.'

Eggars asked, 'How many pirates are there?'

'Twenty or thirty of the bastards, I reckon.'

The steady pulsation of the engines, which normally vibrated through the ship and soon became hardly noticeable, suddenly ended with a convulsive shudder of the hull. We heard a couple of shots beneath our feet and Bedell said, 'They're in the bloody engine room.'

I said, 'Then let's get 'em out of it — show us the way there.'

Grigor, Arthur and Eggars followed as Bedell led us to the steel door to the engine room. Looking past him I saw a body in overalls, splotched with oil and blood, lying on the grating which ran round the top of the machinery area. Bedell muttered, 'That's Harry, Fourth Engineer,' and called, 'You all right, Harry?'

A groaning voice answered, ''Course I'm not bloody all right. The buggers shot the greaser, then made me stop the engines, then shot me in the arse when I tried to get away up the ladders. Hurts like buggery.'

'How many pirates are there?'

'Only two or three.'

I asked, 'Are there any more of our crew down there?'

'No. We're oil-burning. No firemen or trimmers. For Christ's sake help me out.'

On sudden impulse I handed my weapon to Bedell and stepped through on to the grating. I looked down into the space filled with a mass of machinery, glistening with steel, brass and copper surfaces, but couldn't see the pirates. My skin flinched in expectation of a bullet as I stepped across to Harry, and Arthur followed me. We manhandled Harry, cursing and yelping, out on to the deck just as there was a cracking boom from somewhere overhead. Bedell said, 'I'll bet that's the safe in the ship's office! They've blown it open!'

Arthur said, 'Sounds more like they've blown it apart.'

An even larger explosion, from somewhere up forward, caused Bedell to say, 'And that'll be the opium, stowed in a locked compartment in number two hold.'

Harry sniffed loudly, then complained, 'I smell smoke.'

I hadn't noticed Grigor slip away but he seemed to have deserted us. I was thinking it was time I went back to Ana when Harry cried out, 'That *is* smoke! The bloody ship's on fire!'

Bedell told him, 'You'll need to get back down the engine room, then, to start the pumps for the firehoses.'

'How the hell can I do that? Anyway, there's pirates down there.'

Eggars said, 'Arthur and I can stay here — how about you two try to find another engineer.'

I suddenly realized that 'you two' meant Bedell and me. Bedell said 'Righto' and I wanted to return to Ana but felt a duty to the ship. I followed Bedell up to the officers' and engineers' quarters, seeing nothing of the pirates except for a couple of scorched bodies lying outside the wreckage of the ship's office, amidst a scatter of banknotes blown out of the safe. Just after that I told Bedell, 'That's a weird smell,' and he answered, 'That'll be the bloody opium, I reckon — thousands of quids' worth burning up and setting the rest of the cargo afire.'

Nobody stopped us releasing the men locked up by the pirates and Bedell, assuming my co-operation, said, 'Take the chief engineer and the doctor down to the engine room, will you? I'll go and rouse out the crew for firefighting.'

A stream of passengers was moving up to the boatdeck and as we pushed through them I looked for Ana but couldn't see her. We found Eggars and Arthur standing composedly by the engine room door and I saw two bodies outstretched on the grating, whether dead or wounded I couldn't tell. I asked Eggars, 'What happened?', and he replied casually, 'They tried to make a run for it and I potted 'em.'

I felt they were all capable of solving their own problems and returned to my search for Ana, which took me up to the boat-deck. There, I found that the pirates who had survived the clumsy attempt to blow open the ship's safe and blast a way into the opium cargo were trying to lower one of the lifeboats. We learned later they had planned a quick raid and getaway by stealing enough opium to load a couple of the boats and sail away in them.

But inexperience with explosives spoiled this scheme and they had no more success with the boat. Swarms of panic-stricken Chinese passengers were forcing their way up to the boat-deck and joining in a scramble for places in the boats, while the first-class passengers watched helplessly as though waiting for someone to give them priority. But the ship's officers and crew were too busy fighting the fire in number two hold.

I couldn't see Ana amongst the passengers and no one could tell me where she was. I hurried down to our cabin and found it empty, then ran from one cabin to another and found them all abandoned. I strove for self-control as I looked everywhere I could think of. Then, in the dining saloon, I heard muffled voices from the pantry. Its door was closed but the sliding shutter of the serving hatch was open an inch or so. Through the gap I could see Grigor's back as he stood against the serving counter, and I could hear him talking persuasively.

Then I heard Ana say something which seemed to chop off his patience. With sudden urgency he shouted, 'You stupid bitch, don't you understand we can all make a fortune? Just do as I say and — '

Instantly, everything seemed to happen at once. I grabbed the hatch shutter and jerked it back, and saw Ana dodge round Grigor so that she faced me. She didn't notice me because she was intent on several utensils racked on top of the serving counter, including a carving knife.

When she snatched it up I knew what she'd do but she ignored my shout of protest. Grigor, who'd turned side on to me when she dodged past him, tried to push her away from him but he was too late. As agile as a dancer — or a fencer — she evaded him and lunged the knife into him.

The blade must have pierced his aorta. I heard his horrible choking gasp as I pulled the pantry door open and grasped at her just as she jerked the knife out and poised it for another stab. The blood hosed out of him as he bent over and collapsed, missing us but pooling on the pantry floor.

She dropped the knife as I hustled her out of the pantry, and in a high shuddering voice she complained, 'He pulled me in there when I was trying to get to the lifeboats! He kept on saying I look so much like Anastasia I could pretend to be her, and claim my father's money in the Bank of England! He said he'd help me make up the story! Even said my injuries could help because I'd say I got them escaping from the Reds!'

I paused, holding her round the shoulders

and feeling her violent tremors. I listened for a few moments in case anyone was coming but heard only the throbbing of the pumps down in the engine room. Ana asked shakily, 'Do you think he really knows who I am?'

I said, 'No, of course not. I'd better have a look at him.'

Whatever schemes, or knowledge, Grigor might have cherished had now vanished for ever. No one could have lost that much blood and survived. The carving knife lay in it and I picked it up with my handkerchief. Returning to Ana I assured her, 'You won't have to worry about him any more. I'll throw the knife overboard and everyone will think the pirates did for him.'

I felt the vibration of the ship as the engines started again and I said, 'Let's go up on the boat-deck and see what's happening.'

25

Afterwards we heard that a mingled boatload of pirates and Chinese passengers had managed to push off from the ship, but never knew what happened to them. The engineers started the pumps and then the engines, enabling the ship to turn stern to the wind and blow the flames forward, where Bedell and his men fought them. The chief officer assumed command and decided he didn't want to enter Hong Kong with a number of corpses on board. He ordered a single burial ceremony for all of them, Chinese, Sikh and European, and I felt a secret relief when I saw the canvas-wrapped body of Grigor Peskov slide from a hatchboard into the South China Sea.

The *Loh Ning* limped into Hong Kong about a day late. I reported to the Royal Navy base there and received orders to stay in the colony long enough to attend the preliminary enquiry into the incident, held for insurance and other reasons. Ana and I were put up in a nice little hotel, our baggage hadn't been harmed or stolen, and we should have been able to enjoy a pleasant break.

But I was concerned by Ana's reaction to the affair. She had become almost as silent and withdrawn as she had been during our escape from Russia and she was unresponsive to my attempts to reassure her. She seldom left the hotel room and I had to refuse several invitations from my RN contemporaries.

One early evening I made another attempt to persuade her to talk about her worries. Our room opened on to a balcony and she did not resist when I gently guided her out there. For a few minutes we simply gazed at the view, across the magnificent harbour to the camel-coloured hills of China, while I chatted inconsequentially. Then I said gently, 'I hope you're not worried about Grigor. Nobody suspects you and we'll soon be far away from here.'

To my astonishment she burst out with, 'You say you love me but how do I know you're not as bad as he was?'

I spluttered, 'What on earth do you mean?', and she almost shouted, 'Grigor was after my father's money! Is that what you want too?'

I snapped, 'Don't be absurd!', but she yelled, 'Is that what everyone wants? Is that why you rescued me, and married me when I didn't know what was happening, and I had to go through all those horrible operations?'

She started to scream: high hysterical

shrieks which merged into floods of tears. I wrestled her back into the room and on to the bed, where she convulsed wildly. There were no telephones in hotel rooms in those days but I pressed my thumb on the room-service button until a Chinese 'boy' came scampering along, mouth and eyes wide when he saw Ana on the bed though she had stopped screaming and was simply weeping. I told him, 'Get doctor quick!'

He nodded and scurried away but we had to wait a long time for the doctor, a skinny, little old man with glasses so thick his eyes were like blue blurs. Ana was silent and motionless on the bed by that time and when he asked, 'What's the matter?', I told him, 'She's had a bad shock . . . we were in that business on the *Loh Ning*.'

'You'd better leave me with her, then.'

I stood out on the balcony, hearing the mutter of their voices inside the room, and stared blankly at the lights coming on over the city and on ships in harbour. I wondered whether she was confessing to the murder of Grigor but when the doctor at last came out to me he only asked, 'How on earth did she get all those injuries? She only says it was an accident.'

'Well, it was the war. We were in Russia, and . . . '

'Ah, I see. She obviously had a bad time and the pirate attack's had a fairly severe effect. Anyway, I've given her a dose of laudanum to calm her down, and a prescription for more when she needs it. That'll be twenty dollars, plus ten for the medicine.'

When he'd gone, Ana, now in nightie and negligée, gave me a shamefaced smile and murmured, 'I'm so sorry, darling . . . I don't know what made me go on like that.'

Nowadays they would call it something like 'post-traumatic stress disorder', but the language of psychiatry was still being invented. Erratic behaviour was generally described as 'nerves'. Such palliatives as tranquillizers and anti-depressants were unknown.

I answered awkwardly, 'That's all right, darling. I understand. Er . . . would you like some dinner?'

'No, that medicine has made me so sleepy. You go and have yours.'

I was glad to swallow a stiff whisky in the bar. I was gradually relaxing when the ship's doctor from the *Loh Ning* came in, with a couple of shipmates. They joined me and we chatted over a couple of drinks until some girls came in, and the shipmates went over to join them. The doctor said, 'What about some dinner? I'm starving.'

When we'd ordered he asked, 'How's your good lady?'

I gave him a brief and censored account of her 'attack', as I now thought of it. He wagged his head wisely and said, 'Nerves.'

I told him, 'The doctor gave her some laudanum. Is that OK?'

'Certainly. It will relax her and help her sleep.'

'But what is it?'

'Opium dissolved in alcohol. Opium's not illegal in Hong Kong — or not yet, anyway.'

The waiter brought our first course and when we'd started on it he said, 'We British brought opium to China from India, so it's only fair that people should still be allowed to buy it. Properly used, it's a most beneficial drug.'

When I returned to the bedroom I wondered what I'd find, but Ana was sleeping peacefully and did not stir when I slipped in beside her.

The enquiry opened next day and proceeded quickly, serving no useful purpose beyond confirming that the ship had been seized and set on fire by pirates who were subsequently defeated. The local newspaper scolded the British government for failing to order the Royal Navy to blast the pirate hideaways.

Soon after that Ana and I boarded a passenger ship for Sydney. She seemed to have recovered from her attack of 'nerves' though I occasionally saw her measuring out the pale golden drops of laudanum into a glass of water. I was tempted to ask, 'Do you really need that stuff?' but I was afraid she might say something like, 'Yes — it helps me to put up with you.'

I'd been unhappy about the palliative ever since I heard it was opium. Such phrases as 'opium addict' and 'opium dens' drifted through my mind, with images of pigtailed Chinese puffing at opium pipes. Like most people at that time I knew little about drugs of addiction, though I'd heard about wounded soldiers becoming addicted to morphia administered as a painkiller. In fact ignorance was so common, and the regulations so slack, that the producers of a new morphia derivative could market it freely under the name of 'heroin' — because it will make you feel like a hero'. They claimed it wasn't addictive but of course it was, just like the tobacco and alcohol I enjoyed frequently.

But I saw that laudanum kept Ana calm and relaxed, and told myself she'd eventually come to the end of her supplies. She certainly seemed happy enough when our ship sailed into beautiful Sydney Harbour, even when a boatload of journalists came aboard in search of interesting or colourful characters arriving in Australia. That was common practice in those days before broadcast radio and TV, when the country seemed remote from the rest of the world. When the journalists heard we'd been 'pirated' they besieged us for the story, and it received so much coverage that, when I reported at Royal Australian Navy HQ on Garden Island in Sydney Harbour, I was received half-humorously and half-admiringly.

The navy wives, with typical Aussie hospitality, helped Ana to settle in and we found a neat little house on Cremorne Point, overlooking the harbour. The garden ran down to the water's edge and ended in a small landing stage.

The RAN was small but efficient. The 1920s were a time of hope and new beginnings but the Australians were always conscious of the menace of Japan, like a storm cloud beyond the northern horizon. My duty was to help maintain contact between the RN and RAN, exchange ideas and so on. I was away from home occasionally, on cruises or manoeuvres or visiting shore establishments in other parts of Australia, but Ana's new friends helped to keep her happy.

And they launched us into a fairly busy social life, ranging from dances and bridge parties to sailing races on Sydney Harbour. We became honorary members of various clubs and guests in the upper levels of Sydney society. Ana's only problem was her lack of domestic experience. Servants, in those days, were still comparatively cheap and easy to obtain in Britain and Europe, but Australians didn't much fancy the occupation. After some difficulty we found a 'daily cook-general' by the name of Mrs Cassidy, who arrived each morning and left in the evening. She was a hefty middle-aged Irish-Australian, pretty free with opinions about everything.

Ana adapted well to our new lifestyle. Sometimes we talked about having another baby but she was hesitant. We 'took precautions' until we awoke together in a glorious summer dawning and turned to each other in sudden unexpected passion. A few weeks later she told me, apparently unperturbed, that she was pregnant. Her doctor had told her not to worry about her previous stillbirth because, he said, it wouldn't necessarily happen again.

She was in her sixth month when I returned home, late on a Sunday afternoon, from a tennis party she'd declined to attend because 'I'm too heavy to play and too sleepy to watch'. The doors and windows of the house were open to a harbour breeze and she didn't hear me when I padded into the house in tennis shoes, until I stood in our bedroom doorway and saw her measuring golden drops into a little water. She turned, saw me and quickly swallowed the dose. I asked, 'Are you still taking that stuff?'

She said defiantly, 'Yes, I am!'

'But where do you get it?'

'Don't you read the papers?'

She referred to the parliamentary debates about moves to ban the uncontrolled production of opium, which Chinese immigrants brought to Australia in the goldrush era. Some, unsuccessful on the gold fields, began growing opium poppies. Subsequent usage of opium in patent medicines, and sale by illegal dealers, created many addicts.

I said, 'Yes, but who sells it to you?'

I had moved into the room and she seemed to brace herself to face me, eyes staring into mine. 'Mrs Cassidy, if you must know!'

'What! Then she'll have to go!'

'She will not! And I don't use that much of it nowadays!'

I grabbed for the bottle but she snatched it up and held it behind her back. I said, 'But it may harm the baby.'

'Mrs Cassidy says she's known many a girl

have a fine baby while she's on the dope, as she calls it.'

'Rubbish! Here — give me that!'

'Your trouble is you don't understand.'

'Understand what?'

'How it feels to be me! All the memories going round and round in my head and I can't talk to anyone about them. And whenever I meet someone new they say, 'Oh, you're Russian — how interesting! What do you think about that woman who claims to be Anastasia?' and I want to scream out, 'I *am* Anastasia!''

'Maybe you should. Bring it all out in the open.'

'God! Just think what the newspapers would make of that! There'd never be a moment's peace. And anyway . . . ' She drew in a long quivering sigh. 'I'm so afraid of the Bolsheviks . . . that they'll kill me to prevent me becoming a leader of the Whites. Don't you understand why I take laudanum? It helps me push all these things out of my mind . . . '

I took her gently into my arms and she came against me, with the bulk of her pregnancy between us. She whispered, 'What's to become of me?', and I answered, 'I'll look after you.'

Soon after that I had to attend a formal

dinner in the officers' wardroom at HQ. The company included a surgeon-commander with whom I was friendly and, after dinner, I steered the conversation round to the opium legislation. He said, 'It'll be passed all right, as it was last year in Britain.'

'I always think opium must be a weird thing to enjoy.'

He drew on his cigar. 'Tell that to the ancient Egyptians, who discovered it. And the Greeks, who copied them. Homer is supposed to have said, 'Opium bestows forgetfulness of pain and evil.''

I signalled the steward to refill our glasses and asked, 'Can you explain addiction?'

'It's both chemical and psychological. Something in a substance affects the personality of the consumer, and makes them want more of it. Look at morphine, derived from opium. It relieves agonizing pain, and makes you feel optimistic about a cure, but you soon can't do without it. You're happy and cheerful when you've had a dose but depressed and down-hearted when the effect wears off.'

He sipped his brandy and said cheerfully, 'Just like alcohol.'

I thought about all this on the way home and half-expected to find Ana was a gibbering addict. But she looked rosy and happy and greeted me cheerfully, and I reproached myself for thinking that might be the result of a recent dose of laudanum.

For a few weeks all went well. I borrowed a dinghy from Garden Island and kept it moored at the landing stage, and took Ana on sailing trips round the harbour. My duties and our social life kept me pleasantly occupied and my only unease derived from Mrs Cassidy. Sometimes she looked at me with a knowing little smile, as though she knew what had passed between me and Ana. I had to check myself from rapping out, 'What the hell are you grinning at?'

I began to see a change in Ana during the last month of her pregnancy. She looked apprehensive, her colour faded, and she slept poorly. But when I asked her what was wrong she only shook her head, answering, 'Can't say, really, and the doctor doesn't help.'

I asked bluntly, 'Is it that bloody laudanum?'

Her eyes brimmed and overflowed. 'No . . . if it was I'd stop it. But I felt like this just before my last baby, and . . . '

I held her as she sobbed, not knowing what to say. Obstetrical specialists were rare in those days, especially in Australia, but her doctor sent her to some kind of specialist and he reported favourably. He said, 'Everything seems to be proceeding normally and I detect a strong prenatal heartbeat.'

But Ana began to suffer from what I thought of as a truly Russian premonition, mournful and inconsolable.

26

Many babies were still born at home but the fashion was developing for accouchements in nursing homes. One, favoured by Ana's friends, lay not far from us on the harbourside and was run by a Sister Fitzgerald. We made an introductory visit and at one moment we stood in the small ward where our baby would be born. We looked out at the magnificent view, where white sails scudded over blue water, and I put my arm round Ana and said romantically, 'Just think of the time when you and I and the baby look out at this view.'

She smiled faintly but said nothing. Sister Fitzgerald, a large strong lady with a square jaw and a manner as hearty as a stock-rider's, nodded as though to say, 'She'll be all right in my place.'

I was a little less happy when Ana told Mrs Cassidy about the arrangement and she said, 'Aw, yes, you'll be in a good camp there. My niece Bridget works in the kitchens there and she reckons it's a bonzer place.'

At last the morning came when Ana awoke in considerable discomfort. At about midday the doctor had her moved into the nursing home and I expected to be a father that evening. But nothing happened, and when I called in next morning on my way to work I found her weary and apprehensive. She said dully, 'It's just like last time . . .'

I would gladly have given her laudanum, or anything else she wanted, but when I asked if I could do anything for her she only closed her eyes and shook her head.

I returned that evening but Sister Fitzgerald wouldn't let me see Ana, saying briskly, 'The doctor's on his way. We'll let you know when there's any news. Now, I've got four babies trying to get here tonight — '

The phone call didn't come until nearly midnight, when Sister Fitzgerald rang me. She said, 'I think you'd better come round.'

'Why? What's the matter?'

She said only, 'Soon as you can. I'll be in my office.'

Her strong face was weary when she beckoned me in and said, 'Shut the door.' She poured tea from a large thermos, asking, 'Want some?'

I shook my head. 'What's happened to Ana?'

'First, the doctor never made it. A drunk driver rammed his car on his way here, and broke his arm. We had another doctor here but he's been busy with the other deliveries. And the fact is . . . '

She sipped her tea, her eyes not meeting mine.

I said bleakly, 'She's dead.'

'Not your wife. The baby is, though. Stillborn, and never breathed or cried.'

I didn't know what to think or say. She said, 'Ana had a hard time but she's asleep now. I gave her a whiff of chloroform. I'm not supposed to unless the doctor's there but I thought it best. I delivered your baby myself, without even any of the other nurses. They've all been so busy. And now I've got a suggestion.'

She finished her tea, then said, 'Another of the girls having a baby tonight is the daughter of a friend of mine. Her boyfriend put her in the family way and then took off. Know what I mean?'

'Of course.'

'Well, the poor kid's baby is due any moment, and I thought . . . '

She stared at me, allowing her 'thought' to drift from her mind into mine. When I grasped her meaning I stammered, 'But — '

'You'd do everyone a favour. Your poor little wife'll be so upset, having another stillborn, and my friend's daughter would be spared all the shame of . . . bringing up a bastard child.'

Her comment characterized the days when abortion was both sinful and illegal, whereas a fatherless child was also regarded as a sin and often relegated to an orphanage.

I said, 'But surely other people will know about it? The nurses, maybe?'

'Good nurses know how to keep their mouths shut, and mine have worked with me for a long time. Some of us trained together.'

'What about the doctor?'

'The one on duty now has never ever seen the girl before — or seen your Ana. And I'll show him where to sign the certificate.'

The only other question I could think of was, 'What's the . . . er . . . girl's name?'

'Ellen O'Shaughnessy. Good Irish stock. Comes from the country but worked in Sydney, and lives with an aunt. Terrible disgrace for both of them, and they won't argue about a baby born dead.'

A long wailing cry, and a series of sobbing groans, came from somewhere in the building. She stood up, saying, 'I'd better go,' but stared at me almost hypnotically and demanded, 'What do you think, then? Ana will be dopey for a while yet but . . . '

I found myself nodding jerkily. 'Yes, all right.'

plenty of rest because she'd had such a hard time. I never knew whether Sister Fitzgerald told him about the baby swap but I doubt it. Ana was still in hospital when the Admiralty ordered me to terminate my appointment as RAN Liaison Officer and gave me few weeks to do so. British politicians had decided there wouldn't be any more wars and that they could run down the armed forces. But at least I was lucky enough to remain in service, unlike the thousands pushed into civil life. Perhaps Rear-Admiral Blaze was still looking after me.

I began preparing for departure before Ana brought the baby home. One sunny afternoon I was on our little landing stage, preparing the sailing dinghy for return to the RAN, when Mrs Cassidy came down the steep path from the house. She'd been looking after me in fairly slapdash style while Ana was away and when she stepped on to the landing stage I thought she'd have some domestic query. But she simply nodded to me and lit a cigarette, and when I faced her I could smell whisky. She said abruptly, 'I dropped in to see my niece Bridget yes'dy, up the hospital, and looked in on your missus.' She drew deeply on the cigarette, then grinned at me and said, 'I asked did she want some more of that stuff

I sells her but she reckons it might hurt the baby.'

'Good girl.'

She stared challengingly at me as she sucked at her cigarette. 'Yeah. Well, any road, I went down the kitchen to see Bridget and she was the only one there that time of day. And she tells me this story. Know what I mean?'

'Can't say I do.'

'Well, it's like a rumour, see? You know how they get around.'

'I never listen to rumours. They're usually wrong.'

'But this one might be right.'

'Have you got any proof?'

She took a final drag at her cigarette and flicked the butt away. 'Not what you might call proof. The other ... er ... mother's gone back up the country. And Sister Fitzgerald fixed everything about the poor little dead baby. Death certificate, cremation, an' so on.'

'How does Bridget know all this?'

'She reckons she heard two of the nurses talking while they was sorting out the laundry.'

We stared at each, other until she said, 'You wouldn't want it to get in the newspapers. They'd ask all sorts of questions and your missus'd be upset. So proud of her baby, she is.'

'And how much would keep it out of the papers?'

'I reckon a thousand smackers'd cover it.'

I almost burst out laughing. In those days a thousand Australian pounds would have covered her wages for about seven years. But her insolent stare and heartless demand made me snap, 'You're sacked! Get out before I report you for attempted blackmail!'

She jerked her head towards me like a snake striking, and like a snake she hissed, 'You Pommie bastard! Wait till the papers — '

I shoved her away from me, harder than I'd intended. She tottered backwards, swayed on the edge of the landing stage, and fell in. She vanished, but bobbed up spluttering, 'Help! I can't — '

I wore only slacks, a sweater and sandshoes. I jerked off the shoes and dived in after her, but the tide had carried her a little distance away and she vanished again just as I dived. My fingers touched her wet clothing and grabbed at it, but she was struggling frantically and I lost my grip. I surfaced for a gulp of air, dived again, but couldn't find her. The tide had carried me a good way from the landing stage before I gave up trying and struggled back to the stage, and had to sit for a while, gasping for breath, until I staggered up to the house. I glanced around at neighbouring houses overlooking the harbour, and at various craft in the vicinity, but nobody seemed to have noticed anything.

I phoned the police and had time to change my clothes, and think up my story, before a sergeant and constable arrived. I felt certain some witness would turn up but there was no sign of any interest. When the sergeant asked, 'How did it happen?', I said glibly, 'I'm not sure, really. I think she just went a bit too close to the edge and her foot slipped.'

The sergeant stared around as though seeking inspiration. The windows of the houses stared blankly back at us, some yachts cruised along before the wind, and a freighter churned busily across the middle distance. He said, 'The sharks've probably taken her by now.'

He asked a few questions and took some notes but seemed not to have any suspicions. A newspaper reporter rang up later in the day but harbour drownings weren't uncommon and the story rated only a few lines. On my evening visit to the hospital I told Ana about the incident and she expressed formal regret but said airily, 'I must say I never liked her much, and she wasn't even a very good cook.'

Somehow her comment annoyed me and I

found myself thinking: She was the third person I killed for you and you might at least show some gratitude. But of course that was absurd and I said nothing.

Mr Norm Cassidy came to see me and I was oddly surprised to find him a sober and respectable personality, a locomotive driver on the Melbourne Express. When I told him the same story as I'd told the police sergeant he sighed and said, 'There was never no reason for her to go out to work. I make a good wage. But looking after the house and kids was never enough for her and she got . . . restless.'

The body was never found and so there was only a memorial service. I went to this and Mr Cassidy introduced me to Bridget. I'd feared she might spread the story of the baby swap and thus rouse official suspicions, but I found she was a shy and tearful teenager overwhelmed by the family tragedy. Presumably she'd decided there was no point in telling the story to anyone else, or perhaps even dismissed it as mere gossip.

I had to attend the inquest, but I'd become accustomed to giving evidence on such occasions and nobody asked any awkward questions.

After that I couldn't wait to get out of Australia. The shipping companies didn't like to carry babies less than three months old but young Alex, as we'd decided to name our son, had just reached that mark when the liner carrying us homewards steamed out between Sydney Heads.

27

Natasha had no children from her first marriage but she and Billy made up for lost time. Three of their offspring were amongst the occupants of Knyve's Edge and two more, in the form of twins, were on their way. But the old house had plenty of room for all of us, Ana was content to leave the housekeeping to Natasha, and domestic help was still absurdly cheap and easy to obtain.

When my home leave ended I was appointed to an administrative job in the Admiralty, which suited me because I could spend most weekends at home and see young Alex growing through his first couple of years. He was a fine sturdy little fellow with merry blue eyes and a confident grin, much loved and admired by Natasha's family. Sometimes, when I remembered how he came to Ana and me, it seemed absurd to think he was an accidental acquisition. But, as time went by, I seldom gave a thought to that incident.

Ana and I thought he should have a sibling but, after three more miscarriages, we abandoned that idea. Doctors in those days seemed rather vague about the causes and cures for such happenings and they blamed Ana's on her 'war injuries'.

Those days when I was climbing the ladder seemed to pass with hurricane speed. After the Admiralty job I went through a series of courses in gunnery, destroyers, aircraft carriers, and so on. Then I spent a couple of years as a lecturer at Dartmouth Naval College, followed by a year's stint as naval attaché to the British Embassy in Washington. I was beginning to wonder if I'd ever get back to sea when, with the rank of commander, I became second-in-command of a cruiser in the Mediterranean Fleet. This two-year commission was followed by a similar appointment in the Home Fleet.

The Great Depression of 1929-34 had its effect on us as on so many other people. The Knyves, like other families whose income came directly or indirectly from the land, had already suffered from the agricultural depression of the 1920s but Billy's skilful management, supported by Natasha, enabled the estate and its farms to weather a storm which bankrupted many others.

Ana and Alex were able to accompany me on my various appointments until, at the age of eight and much to Ana's annoyance, he went as a boarder to an English preparatory school. This was an essential move if he wanted, as he had proclaimed since the age of six, to follow me into the Royal Navy. When he was thirteen facing the selection board for Dartmouth, he possessed the physique, intelligence and confident good nature which virtually guaranteed acceptance. It was strange to think, though, that the seventh-generation Knyve to become a naval officer was quite possibly descended from one of the Irish rebels transported to Australia a century earlier.

By the time Alex graduated from the training cruiser, and sported the white patches of a midshipman on his lapels, I wore the four gold rings of a captain on the sleeves of my uniform jackets and held a staff position, based on Malta, in the Mediterranean Fleet.

A good many officers' wives, including Ana, lived on Malta while their husbands occupied various positions ashore or afloat. I felt there was little danger of anyone thinking she was Anastasia Romanov. Apart from the physical changes, including those of maturing into the late thirties, she had fitted herself smoothly into the role of a naval officer's wife and lady of the English upper classes. Only an occasional touch of Russian accent — and temperament — might betray her.

As for the 'false' Anastasia, the media had largely lost interest in her though she kept on trying to prove herself until her death in 1984. Later, DNA tests proved she was not a Romanov.

Ana had her first heart attack on Malta, during a tennis party. I'd noticed her rubbing her chest that morning but when I'd asked, 'What's wrong?', she answered, 'Just muscle strain, I think.' But the pain hit that afternoon and she was rushed to hospital. Doctors were still fairly ignorant about heart problems and many patients became bedridden, but Ana refused to accept such a fate. She insisted on resuming normal activities, and although the experience slowed her down a little she managed to survive it.

A few months later she packed up for our return to England. I'd been given command of the new light cruiser *Artemis*, which was about to leave the builder's hands. War broke out during our shakedown cruise, giving extra impetus to the task of slotting 632 men into their shipboard duties. We were ready for service before Christmas and we'd sailed for the Mediterranean when Italy joined Germany in 1940.

We spent the next three years in the Mediterranean: a time in which I felt completely fulfilled. I'd spent my life preparing for an active service command and the *Artemis* was a fine ship to combat the king's enemies. Wickedly fast and manoeuvrable, she could deliver a torpedo attack while fighting off aircraft and pouring sixty-four six-inch shells a minute into an enemy ship or position. Of course we received our share of black eyes but nothing the dockyard at Alexandria couldn't deal with.

Ana settled in with Natasha and Billy for the war years, which soon restored prosperity to agriculture. Her heart problem gave her a few spells in hospital but she refused to be invalided.

Alex seemed to find the war years as professionally satisfying as I did. He began them with convoy duty in the North Atlantic, that arena where thousands of Royal and Merchant Navy seamen died. Next came a period in command of a Motor Torpedo Boat, harassing shipping on the enemy coast. After that he volunteered for submarines, took the wartime course, and became torpedo officer in a new S-class submarine.

On spells of home leave he sailed through a typical wartime affair. On one leave he met Sheila Allenby, a Women's Land Army girl working on the Home Farm and living with our family. On the next leave they became engaged, on the third they were married, and on the fourth he made her pregnant before his submarine left home waters to join the war against Japan.

I first met Sheila and her baby in September 1943, when I brought the *Artemis* home for a refit and found a nation very different from the one I'd left. The atmosphere was cheerful and optimistic, accepting of hardships and determined to win. I arrived at Knyve's Edge during harvest and found no one had much time to spare for me. Every inch of suitable ground — even along the roadsides — had been sown to wheat and the golden grain rippled in breezes from the sea. I joined in the work and found it an agreeable change from bombarding German shore positions in Italy.

Much of the time I worked alongside Sheila, who left her baby Robert — generally known as Bobby — in Ana's care while she worked in the harvest fields. She was a fine handsome girl with hair as blonde as the ripe wheat. Sometimes we chatted as we worked and on one occasion she remarked, 'Alex doesn't look much like you and Ana, does he? He's got what I think of as Gaelic colouring — black hair, blue eyes, white skin.'

I passed that off with a joking, 'Probably there's an Irish adventurer somewhere in the family background,' just as Ana appeared with a lunch basket on one arm and one-year-old Bobby on the other. I watched him while we ate and he waved wheatstalks at sparrows foraging for crumbs. I thought he had very English colouring, with grey eyes, pink cheeks and brown hair, but I asked Ana, 'Who d'you think Bobby looks like?'

She flashed me the kind of glance reserved for askers of awkward questions, but Sheila said cheerfully, 'I think he looks like my late Great Uncle Edgar, who was a very naughty old man.'

I laughed politely at that, but there'd been something in Ana's look which stuck in my mind. As though by mutual unspoken agreement we never talked about Mrs Cassidy, Sister Fitzgerald, or any other details of the day or two in which she was trying to deliver her own child, but I'd often wondered whether Ana really believed that Alex was her son. I found it hard to believe she could be deceived but I was always glad she accepted the situation.

The beautiful late summer merged into autumn and I felt myself relaxing in my home country. Ana seemed content with the domestic and countrywoman's duties she'd accepted though I saw a bluish tinge in her cheeks and sensed she was pacing herself. I didn't know, until much later, she'd had a couple of serious heart attacks while I was away. The family had decided not to worry me by telling me about them while I was on active service.

My leave ended, I rejoined the *Artemis*, and found we were to serve in the escort of convoys to Murmansk in northern Russia. On our first assignment we escorted the British section of a 'Russian convoy' from Loch Ewe to Iceland, where we joined the American-Canadian section. A total of forty-eight ships laden with war materials sailed from the North Atlantic into the Arctic Ocean, along the northern coasts of Norway and Russia where the Germans had strong air-sea bases. The convoys had two deadly enemies: the savage winter storms and the determined attacks by German ships, aircraft and U-boats. But Murmansk was the only Russian port open to the Allies and the convoys fought their way through.

The *Artemis* suffered only minor damage until 1944. On a fairly mild spring day, with a long swell rolling between horizons hidden in light mist, we were only a day's steaming from Murmansk when our radar picked up an intruder approaching from the south. I'd just ordered 'Action Stations' when the intruder began firing by radar. We heard the muffled thud-thud-thud of her guns and a salvo burst well short of us. We responded, and a minute or so later she seemed suddenly to leap out of the mist. She was a light cruiser of the *Emden* class, a fair match for the *Artemis* and capable of doing immense damage to the convoy if she could batter her way past us. I saw the flash of a broadside and within a couple of minutes both ships were aflame as we scored hit after hit on each other.

I was in my usual action station on the forebridge, with the usual group of officers, petty officers and ratings. I'd just ordered a change of course when I heard a colossal rushing whirr, the sound of an incoming shell. I tried to shout a warning but the shell exploded before I could speak.

28

I came to lying on my back, in a strange muffled silence. The first lieutenant and the surgeon-lieutenant were bending over me, amongst the hideous human and inhuman wreckage of the forebridge. I saw their lips move but couldn't hear anything, until hearing suddenly returned with all the sounds of a ship moving at speed. But there was no gunfire and when I gasped ' . . . enemy?' the answer was, 'On fire and sinking. Well astern.'

' . . . us?'

'Fires under control. No damage below waterline, plenty above. Sixty to seventy casualties.'

My uniform was slashed into rags and my body felt as though it had been through a cement mixer, but we later found the damage was restricted to numerous cuts, burns and bruises. But I was subject to bouts of deafness and dizziness, though the surgeon-lieutenant said cheerfully I'd improve as the results of shock faded away. The Murmansk port facilities were subject to frequent German bombing and we set all hands to patching up the damage to *Artemis*, hoping to speed our departure from this dangerous port. We'd been toiling away for about a week when I was told that a Commissar Stasanowski had arrived alongside and had asked to see me.

Of course I remembered the name of Stasanowski and I invited him aboard. He was a big man, fair-haired and with a bristling moustache, who spoke passable English and introduced himself as Commissar Aleksandr Stasanowski. This seemed to strike a chord in my still rather befuddled mind, but we studied each other for a few moments before he said, 'I have a feeling we've met before.'

I shook my head. 'I haven't been in Russia for a quarter-century. You'd have been a boy in those days.'

His face seemed to light up and he asked, 'And you don't remember a boy named Sasha?'

I exclaimed, 'Sasha! Of course I know you!'

Fortunately my supply of Scotch had escaped destruction and we were able to toast our meeting in good whisky. Then he said, 'First to business. We now know the German ship you fought was abandoned by her crew and sunk before they could reach port. The Soviet government wishes to acclaim this victory by bestowing on you the Order of Lenin, and wishes also to decorate ten of your ship's company. You will kindly nominate them.'

I thanked him, and explained I would have to obtain Admiralty permission for acceptance. We discussed that for a few minutes and then I said, 'Tell me what happened after I last saw you.'

He told me that Maria and her brother had adopted him and given him the family surname. Somehow they survived the post-war massacres and famines and Sasha eventually returned to school, and did well enough to be accepted into government service. He concluded, 'And now I have sons of my own!'

But then he frowned, and said, 'Maria talked sometimes about our escape from the Urals. Late in her life she sometimes — well, took too much to drink, and on one of those times she said the girl you married was really the Grand Duchess Anastasia. Could that be true?'

I asked easily, 'Do you think it is?'

He shrugged his big shoulders. 'So many strange things have happened. I've never spoken of this to anyone else because it could have caused trouble for Maria. But you do have a wife?'

'Indeed I do, and she is Russian, and her name was Anastasia Romanov. Both are common enough names in Russia, so maybe Maria became confused in her . . . well, old age.'

He nodded, glanced at his watch, and said, 'Must go. Too much to do.'

He left me with questions churning around in my mind. Had Maria ever told the Soviets about my marriage to Ana? If she had, would they do anything about it? Did Sasha believe the way I'd shrugged off his query?

But such questions seemed of little consequence in comparison with the gargantuan struggle of Russia against Germany. We plunged into it again when we left Murmansk, as one of the escorts of a homebound convoy, but the Germans tended to reserve their main efforts against ships bound for Murmansk with full cargoes. My principal problem was that of recurrent deafness. I became familiar with the politely controlled expressions of my officers when I couldn't hear them properly.

Our voyage ended in an east coast dockyard for completion of repairs. I was able to take a spell of leave and I hoped familiar surroundings would help restore me to normality. For the first three days all went well, especially since little Bobby seemed pleased to see his grandfather. On the fourth afternoon he was so excited by a boat trip on the harbour he fell asleep in my arms on the way home, and Natasha met me as I carried him into the garden. She wore an expression which made me ask, 'What's wrong?'

'Sheila's had a telegram from the Admiralty about Alex, saying he's missing in action.'

Usually that had only one meaning for submariners. I said, 'Oh, my God,' and then, 'How's Sheila taking it? And Ana?'

'Sheila's keeping her chin up. Ana's not too well, I'm afraid. I've been trying to get the doctor but he's so busy these days.'

My hearing had been fairly normal since I reached home but now it seemed to fade in and out. I concentrated fiercely on hearing Ana when I found her huddled on her bed, her face with a greyish tinge. I sat beside her on the bed and we talked for a couple of minutes. I realized she'd given up hope for Alex and with a foolish notion of consoling her I said, 'Darling, he wasn't really ours, you know. He was only — '

She interrupted me with, 'Oh, my dear, I've always known that. I knew our baby was stillborn, before Sister Fitzgerald gave me a bit of anaesthetic. She must have thought I was still unconscious when she brought Alex to me, but I was just coming round.'

For a minute she lay with closed eyes, then she murmured, 'I thought it was so sweet of her to try to save me another disappointment, and Alex was such a dear little baby . . . it was easy to love him as much as if he'd been ours.' Then she said, 'You know my poor little brother was a bleeder — a haemophiliac. Long after those devils killed him I heard the girls of a haemophiliac family don't become bleeders but often have miscarriages. Perhaps that was my real problem . . . '

Her voice faded and I thought she was asleep, and sat with her until Natasha brought the doctor. I left the room while he examined her and waited outside, and only a few minutes passed before he came out and said, 'She's gone, I'm afraid.'

If I hadn't been a naval officer, trained almost since childhood to control my emotions, I might have let out an anguished cry. But I only nodded jerkily, then realized he was saying something more. I saw his lips moving but there seemed to be an invisible wall of silence between us.

And so it has been ever since. Navy doctors and civilian specialists said there was no reason why I shouldn't regain my hearing and that, although the explosion had caused some damage, I should gradually improve. When I did not they mumbled about 'war neurosis', and sent me to a psychiatrist, but I managed to evade his written questions. If I'd started talking where would I have stopped?

The war was over by the time I was invalided out of the navy. Hearing aids never worked for me but I learned lip reading, which is fine if you're facing an interlocutor. But I was cut off from birdsong, music, children's laughter, and all other sweet sounds. Perhaps it's my punishment for doing away with Stefan, Emery Porteous and Mrs Cassidy. But they would have had no mercy on her and killing them was the only way to save Ana from unhappiness.

Now, my life seems to have stretched endlessly on. I've lived in three centuries and everyone I knew has left me behind. Sheila didn't want Bobby to join the navy and he joined the army instead, and died as CO of his unit on the Falklands. He had married, and his son, Martin, is now a lawyer in Norwich.

And now Sheila, also, has gone. I have grand-nephews and grand-nieces, and great-grand ditto, scattered here and there, but have long since lost touch with all of them.

Of course the world has changed around me, as it always changes for everyone. The sleepy little port of Fowlers Haven has become a tourist resort and tourists infest the countryside. Taxation, and other problems, enforced the sale of Knyve's Edge and its farmlands. The old house, with many modifications, became the retirement home where I live now, using my deafness as an excuse not to discuss the family history with other residents.

I suppose that, like many other people, I don't want to leave this world without making some mark on it. Perhaps that's why I've written this narrative. Or, more likely, it's because I miss Ana unceasingly, and this is an attempt to call her back to me.

29

Martin Knyve, a busy solicitor, took several months to absorb his great-grandfather's narrative. After that he locked the manuscript in his safe and tried not to let thoughts of it spoil the pleasure which he, and his family, took in their busy social life. It would be nice to claim relationship with the Russian royal family but everything might be spoiled if people knew he was descended from a sluttish Irish-Australian.

About a year later he received a phone call from a man who introduced himself as Roman Stasanowski. In good though accented English, the caller asked, 'Perhaps you've heard my name before?'

With lawyerly caution Martin answered, 'Possibly.'

Roman would not discuss his business over the phone and so Martin, intrigued by the call, agreed to meet him that evening in his suite in the best hotel in Norwich. He found Roman to be a big handsome man of about forty, who poured whiskies while explaining he was Sasha Stasanowski's only grandson. Sasha's two sons, both army officers, had died in Afghanistan. Sasha himself had lived to a good age and Roman eventually became his executor. 'He'd been an important official, but he didn't leave much except some interesting papers.'

Martin asked, 'And are you an official too?'

'Oh no. Just a businessman. Import and export.'

He handed a sheaf of papers to Martin, saying, 'Old Sasha wrote an account of his meeting with Lieutenant Knyve, the rescue of a girl believed to be Anastasia Romanov, their escape from the Urals and the lieutenant's marriage to Anastasia, and so on. After that, Sasha met Benjamin Knyve in Murmansk during the war, and it seems that prompted him to follow the story by tracking down the descendants of Benjamin and Ana. Do you know anything about this?'

Again Martin answered, 'Possibly.'

He glanced at the papers, which meant nothing to him because they were written in Russian. Roman then produced an envelope full of photostats, saying, 'These are some of the fruits of Sasha's research. Extracts from official registries, certificates of birth, marriage and death and so on.'

'However did he get hold of all of those? And why?'

'As I said, he was an important official

— in the days when the Soviets had representatives everywhere. As for his reasons, I thought he was trying to discover what really happened to Anastasia and what the Soviet Union should do about it. Then I found these.'

Roman handed several more photostats to Martin. They were of a variety of documents in Russian or English or both languages, all dated late in 1914. Martin browsed through them carefully, then said, 'I've heard about this. These from the Bank of England show Emperor Nicholas deposited a lot of money from his personal wealth.'

'Correct. After the war, the White Russians claimed it had been only a guarantee of good faith, and should be returned to any surviving members of the Romanov family. But the Reds said it had been deposited to enable Nicholas and his family to escape to England, and it should now be returned to the Soviets. The bank hung on to the money while they argued about it.'

'This here is a receipt for one million twenty-rouble gold pieces. What would that have been worth!'

'In 1914, about two and a quarter million pounds — at a time when you could build a battleship for a million pounds.'

Martin asked, 'So what's happened to the money?'

'The Soviet Union made several attempts to reclaim it but the bank fended them off, saying it was a personal deposit by Nicholas. Various relations of the imperial family have tried to lay claim to the money but the bank always says there's no proof that all members of the emperor's family died in 1918, and that there might be direct descendants still alive.'

'But haven't there been legal challenges?'

Roman nodded towards the photostats in Martin's hand, saying, 'Yes, but they didn't have this kind of evidence and so they didn't get very far.'

'Then how did Sasha get hold of it?'

'I presume his researchers unearthed them in Soviet government departments.'

'So where are the originals?'

'In a safe place.'

Frowning, Martin leafed through the photostats again before asking, 'Does anyone else know about this?'

'I have some . . . associates, yes. Some of the old Soviets knew about the situation and they were trying to intervene. I needed some help in dealing with them.'

Martin thought it best not to ask what manner of 'help' it had been. Instead, he said, 'I presume that's why it's taken you so long to contact me about this. Sasha must have died years ago.'

Roman simply nodded. Martin said, 'And I suppose you're approaching me, as Anastasia's descendant, to help claim the money.'

'Naturally.'

'What would the gold roubles be worth now?'

'The gold content of the coins would be worth about a hundred and fifty million US dollars. And the compound interest payable by the bank, after nearly a century, would be astronomical.'

Martin handed the photostats back to Roman, asking, 'And what . . . er . . . fee would you be expecting?'

'Fifty per cent. We've had heavy expenses already and there would be more to come. The bank won't give in without a long legal and even political struggle.'

Martin gave him a regretful smile. 'Well, I'm sorry to say your expenses, and efforts, have been in vain. I'm not a direct blood descendant of the Romanovs. I understand their DNA was isolated a number of years ago, from remains discovered in the mineshafts where the Reds threw their corpses, and so the bank's lawyers could demand DNA evidence of my relationship. We couldn't give it, and so that's that.'

Roman asked, 'But what if we could prove that Anastasia adopted your grandfather,

Alex, as her legal son and heir?'

Martin scoffed, 'What rubbish! You don't expect me to — '

'Never mind what I expect. What's your legal opinion?'

'Well, it would certainly alter the case, but — '

'So have a look at these.'

Roman extracted two more photostats from his briefcase, saying, 'As you've seen, Sasha's researchers looked for material in Britain and Australia as well as Russia. I expect they found the originals of these in the old Somerset House materials.'

Martin found the photostats were of documents dated 15 July 1925, signed by Anastasia Knyve with two witnesses and with imposing seals. He scanned the clauses, then said, 'But I doubt whether these documents have any validity. They don't seem to follow any of the requirements of the Child Adoption Act — '

Roman interrupted, 'Which didn't exist in 1925.'

'What?'

'We're advised that Britain, unlike most European nations, didn't have a Child Adoption Act until 1926. Before that, adoption was a hit-and-miss affair and rarely documented. But you'll notice that both witnesses to this document sign themselves LLB, which means they were solicitors. They would have done it correctly.'

Martin nodded agreement, as Roman continued, 'Though we don't understand why Anastasia should have adopted Alex in England when he was born in Australia and his birth was registered there. And why wasn't her husband's name also on the adoption document?' Martin explained briefly, and Roman chuckled at the story and said, 'Now at last I understand several things. And you still have this manuscript by old Captain Knyve?'

'Yes indeed. In his own writing.'

'Then I'm sure our solicitors can make good use of it.'

Roman poured more drinks while he asked Martin, 'So, will you go along with us? My colleagues and I are prepared to meet all the costs, repayable if we win.'

Martin sipped his whisky while thoughts coursed through his mind. He found he wasn't interested in the acquisition of great wealth. He was a partner in a prosperous firm, he enjoyed a comfortable income and a happy family, and as a lawyer he had seen some of the problems caused by sudden riches.

But Roman's proposal, whether won or lost, offered the colour, romance, drama and excitement which, all at once, seemed lacking in his life. He pictured himself as the central character in a challenging trial, calmly fencing with notable barristers. And suddenly he thought: Dammit, if we win I'll buy back Knyve's Edge, and restore it to what it used to be.

He found Roman was watching him intently, and smiled cheerfully at him. 'All right,' he said. 'Let's do it!'

We do hope that you have enjoyed reading this large print book.

Did you know that all of our titles are available for purchase?

We publish a wide range of high quality large print books including:
Romances, Mysteries, Classics
General Fiction
Non Fiction and Westerns

Special interest titles available in large print are:
The Little Oxford Dictionary
Music Book
Song Book
Hymn Book
Service Book

Also available from us courtesy of Oxford University Press:
Young Readers' Dictionary
(large print edition)
Young Readers' Thesaurus
(large print edition)

For further information or a free brochure, please contact us at:
Ulverscroft Large Print Books Ltd.,
The Green, Bradgate Road, Anstey,
Leicester, LE7 7FU, England.
Tel: (00 44) 0116 236 4325
Fax: (00 44) 0116 234 0205